THE BAKERY BY THE COVE

ELLEN JOY

To my beautiful wanderlust cousin, Darcy.

Click HERE or visit ellenjoyauthor.com for more information about Ellen Joy's other books.

CHAPTER 1

*A*lly Williams leaned up against her apartment's front door as Jean-Paul whispered in her ear. With a twist of the knob, she opened the door, stumbling backward into her apartment as she scuffed at her shoes, losing height as they slipped off. Jean-Paul held onto her, pulling her up to his lips and kissing her. Through the open drapes, half of the eighteenth arrondissement could see the two of them.

"Tu es belle," Jean-Paul's thick French accent still made her knees wobble every time he spoke, even though half the time she still didn't know what he was saying. Two years in Paris, and her French still needed a little help with sweet nothings in her ear. Every cell in her body exploded as his breath warmed her earlobe. The French poetry she couldn't understand was suddenly the most beautiful thing she had ever heard as he kissed her.

Then her phone rang.

She disregarded the ringing and kissed him back. He pulled her closer as the phone rang again. He dropped his head, resting his hand on the wall.

"Ignore it," she commanded, kissing him again.

But he stopped. His breathing heavy. "Turn it off."

She slipped beneath his arm and moved toward her purse. Her hands fumbled for the phone and it lit up the inside of her bag with a text from her stepfather, Frank.

911

Her heart pounded for a completely new reason than the look Jean-Paul was giving her. Frank had never texted 911 before. She pulled her shoulders back, suddenly self-conscience, as though her stepfather would be able to see her through the phone. She punched in the number.

"Ally, it's your dad." Her heart dropped.

"What's going on?" Jean-Paul leaned against the wall.

"He's had a heart attack." Frank's voice cracked. "You need to come home."

Michael Mailloux had been happy to help Frank and David. The summer season in Camden Cove could be a nightmare if you were short staffed, not to mention if you were missing your head chef. He'd got the call in the middle of the night. Not that he minded. His current boss, Jack, asked him if he could help out. Jack had been good to him, giving him a job at The Fish Market when he returned home from his deployment. Not too many people took a chance on a guy like him. Reputation is everything in a small town, and Michael's had been worse than bad before he left. The Purple Heart he earned didn't change anyone's perspective. It certainly didn't matter to him. He would always be that kid who was trouble, the son of Mike Mailloux Sr., who left his wife and kid and stole half the town's money in the process.

La Patisserie would be like any other place he'd worked, except instead of cooking, he'd be baking. And Michael enjoyed the baking, a lot. Guys from his squadron would give him a hard time if they knew he could bake a cake better than Martha Stewart. A Marine who baked delicate pastries was a target for sure, but he didn't care. Something about the process, the precision of adding ingredients, carefully folding the batter instead of whisking, the delicate layering of pastries, along with the finishing touches to make the whole treat, was calming. Not that he'd admit it to anyone.

When he arrived at the bakery, at three in the morning no less, Jack met him at the back door.

"I can't thank you enough for this." Jack looked as though he hadn't slept at all.

"How's he doing?"

"He got out of surgery a couple hours ago, so it's touchy for the next twenty-four, but hopefully he's going to be okay."

Michael nodded and followed Jack inside.

He liked David, even admired him. The *I don't give a darn* manner in which he lived his life had been a relief, in a community that judged Michael for an act he hadn't committed. In a small town like Camden Cove, it didn't matter if his father stole the money and ruined others' lives, including his own. They saw the name, and trust was never given.

"I can help, but I'm afraid baking isn't my specialty." Jack walked around, turning on the lights inside the pristine kitchen.

A baker's dream kitchen, no doubt about it. It didn't surprise him that David kept a kitchen like this. Everything was in order, the shelves arranged meticulously. Bowls were nested by size, cooking sheets stacked together like Legos, and every gadget and utensil hung from a brass rack. Was his standing mixer polished? Most chefs only dreamt of a kitchen like this.

"I'm happy to help." Michael rubbed his hands against the cold marble countertop of the island. "Where should I start?"

Jack grabbed a white binder. Papers haphazardly protruded from inside the ringed pages. "David has most of the menu in this." He handed it over to Michael. "But good luck finding his recipes."

Michael opened the cover. Notes on post-its, papers dusted with flour, and scribbled recipes filled the pages. He could hardly read the writing. The notebook was such a juxtaposition to David's kitchen, Michael didn't believe it. "Is this it?"

"I'm afraid so." Jack's forehead creased. "Are you sure you can do it?"

Michael flipped through the loose pages. "I'll be good."

Jack's shoulders immediately relaxed and he let out a sigh. "Thanks, man. I really owe you."

Michael reached out his hand and shook it hard. "Not a problem."

Jack cocked his thumb behind him. "I'll start prepping out front and get it ready to open. Kate should be here soon to work the counter."

Michael looked around the room. He had no idea what he was doing. "Sounds good."

Ally landed in Boston on time. She managed to get a direct flight out of Paris, which had been quicker, even with the two-hour drive added in, than flying into Portland. Her mother met her at the baggage claim and embraced her.

"How is he?" Ally held onto her her.

"They say he's going to be okay." Elise squeezed Ally. "He's lucky to be alive."

Ally only let go to grab her mother's arm. She looked around, watching the other passengers head toward the baggage carousel. She rubbed her eyes with her free hand, the exhaustion of being up for twenty-four hours suddenly hitting her.

"You should try sleeping on the way back," Elise said, pushing the wisps of hair from Ally's eyes like she had when she was little.

Ally suddenly felt like a kid again, with her mother giving her a direct order to take a nap at any sign of sleepiness.

"I'm fine." Sleep had been the cure-all for everything in Ally's life. Under the weather? Did she get enough sleep? Nervous about an exam? She should go to bed early. Early signs of crow's feet? Try taking a nap.

"You look drained."

"Mom, my dad just had a heart attack."

"He's going to be okay." She patted Ally's arm. "David should have taken time to rest, long ago."

"How's Frank?" Ally wondered how her stepfather was handling the whole situation. He tended to fall on the opposite of the spectrum from Elise. He was probably freaking out.

"Well, you know Frank."

Ally nodded. He was freaking out.

"Mostly, the problem is the bakery." They walked up to the silver baggage carousel. "David's going to be in recovery for a few months, at least."

"What?" Ally turned to face her mother. "A few months?"

Suddenly, things became more serious. Yes, he'd had a heart attack, but the doctors had said there was a good outlook. A few *months?*

"He just had open-heart surgery." Elise gave her daughter a look. "He's going to have to take time to recover."

Ally hadn't really thought about recovery time. She figured she'd help out for a few weeks while he got better, but not a few months.

"Don't worry, your cousin Jack set up someone from his restaurant for now, but I'm sure they're going to have to hire someone."

Elise didn't say it, though it floated around them in the air like the aroma of skunk. Ally would be the perfect option.

But Ally had Paris, her own gig at La Patisserie Michalak. Then there was Jean-Paul. His French poetry echoed in her head. What would happen with Jean-Paul if she were to stay so long in Camden Cove? He certainly wasn't going to wait around. But she knew her father wouldn't want just anyone to come into his kitchen. "I can't."

"Of course not." Elise shook her head. "No one thinks you should."

That was *exactly* what everyone was thinking. She was a pastry chef, just like her father, after all. She grew up at the bakery watching him make those pastries, went to the same culinary school in Montreal, even went to Paris like him to become an understudy. Jean-Paul's understudy, as it turned out.

Jean-Paul wasn't someone she wanted to make wait for her. And he was someone she couldn't wait to get back to. She didn't want to spend any longer in this antiquated town than she had to. No, staying for a few months wasn't an option.

Elise pulled off the highway and took the exit to Camden Cove. Time seemed to slow down as they drove through town. So many of the structures and buildings looked exactly the same, but somehow different. The season felt off to her, as though by coming in the peak of summer, she was a tourist in the traffic jam at the one stoplight in town.

She remembered a sign on the wall in the local tavern. "Summer people, and some are not." She always felt she was not. She was a local, just like her family, part of the town, but as the buildings passed by her, she felt a tinge of sadness that she was no longer one of them.

"We're going to stop by David's and pick up a few things for him, then head to the hospital." Elise pulled up to Ally's father's house, the one thing that hadn't changed in Camden Cove. The eighteenth-century colonial looked like it was the set of a film for a regency romance. Her father and his husband had renovated the Georgian house when they moved in together after her parents' divorce. They spent all winter tearing room after room apart. Ally was covered in drywall dust for months... and resentment. When Ally stayed there, she always felt like a visitor at a museum. Expensive art, French décor, statues and crystal *everything*. Porcelain vases, polished silver frames, decorative plates, you name it. Not the kind of place where you could scarf down a bag of potato chips on the couch in front of the television.

Not that she hated going. The food at her dads' was much better than at her mom's place. Which was why everyone assumed David had been her inspiration, but it had been Elise's willingness to let Ally run the kitchen that really got her baking. Her Dad didn't want to give up control. She'd ask him to show her a recipe and he'd say that he'd teach her, but from beginning to end, he'd do it all as she stood and watched. Then she'd go home and do it herself.

Her mom always said it was because she and David were so much alike that they didn't always see eye to eye. Maybe they were? She loved her dad, she did. But the moment David and Elise announced they were getting a divorce her whole life shattered.

Elise and she moved back to the states right away with David and Frank following behind a few months after. Dealing with a new school, a new culture, then being bounced from Elise's to David was hard enough, but when David brought Frank to the old traditional town, it had been more than hard on Ally. Ally learned every horrific vocabulary word that one could use to refer to her father, or Frank, or her, or their relationship. The kids in school had been cruel.

One day, after a boy had said something horrible, she went home and picked up the flour, and the measuring cups. Grabbed a few eggs, some sugar, brown as well, then she took a chocolate bar and chopped it into pieces.

She baked ever since.

Ally hung out in the kitchen as Elise ran upstairs to grab his things. She walked around her dads' house, checking out the changes that had happened over the past year. New things. Frank was always adding antique knick-knacks. It also smelled different. Unfamiliar. Did her room still look the same?

Feeling like an intruder, she snuck up the back staircase and down the hall, tiptoeing as though she were sneaking into a stranger's house. She opened her bedroom door. It creaked at the exact same spot it always did, which made her glad. But then she looked inside. The room was the same, with the same furniture, same arrangement, same posters hanging on her walls, except the room was filled with stuff. Vases, cooking sheets, wrapping paper, puzzle boxes and children's toys, books—lots and lots— and four portable hanging closets in the middle of the floor. When was the last time she had come up here? Had she not stayed with her Dad and Frank during her cousin, Elizabeth's wedding?

"Ally!" Elise called from downstairs. "Where are you?"

Ally grabbed the charm bracelets from her jewelry box and called back, "I'm coming!"

They jumped back in the car and headed off to the hospital and Frank met them outside.

He embraced Ally in a bear hug, holding on longer than usual. "I'm so glad you could get back so soon. He's going to be happy to see you."

She could hear Frank tearing up.

"No problem." She didn't want to display emotion in the front parking lot, so she plastered a smile on her face.

"Let's go upstairs," Elise suggested. "I'm sure David's dying to see you."

Frank gave her a look.

"Oh!" Elise's eyes widened.

From outside the room, Ally could hear the beeping of machines. It wasn't until she saw David that she really under- stood the severity of the situation. That's when her emotions swept over her, but she quickly reined them in when David's emotions poured out. She hadn't really ever seen her dad cry. Once, when the Red Sox won the World Series, or when a dog was killed in a movie, but rarely did David Williams shed a tear. So, when she saw a tear slide down his face, she knew she had to keep it together for the both of them.

"If you wanted me to come home, you could've just asked," she joked, which broke the ice. Williamses didn't show emotions that made anyone uncomfortable. They were seafarers. She leaned over and gave him a hug, causing Frank to jump in the middle and pull her away.

"He shouldn't be moving."

"Hey, Ally Bear." He hadn't used her nickname in years. "Next time I'll call."

His words came out weak and scratchy. His face was pale. Her father's full head of hair looked sparse and grayer. For the first time in her life, her father looked weak. She rubbed his shoulder and felt his warmth.

"Glad you're back," he whispered, reaching his hand to hers.

She choked down the lump in her throat before she let go.

"You two should sit." Frank pushed a chair over to Ally, fussing on everyone, as usual. He scraped a chair over from the other side of the room. "Elise, here."

Elise sat down, but Ally didn't sit, she stood next to David's bed and took his hand. "What do you need? I can take care of the bakery."

"There's no need." Frank shook his head. "Jack asked his sous chef, Michael, and he's happy to fill in until David's better."

Something inside Ally's stomach dropped like a steel drum plummeting from the sky. "Well, I can help."

"Yes, but we didn't want to make you do that," Frank said, pushing the chair closer to her. "Here."

Ally kept standing. "But I can help."

"What about your job with Jean-Paul?" Elise asked.

"Jean-Paul completely understands." The words came out of her mouth before she knew what she was saying. She didn't want to stay here. Jean-Paul wouldn't be that understanding. She didn't want to work in a town that had brought her mostly misery. But she didn't like the idea of them not even asking her. It was as if they hadn't even thought of her.

"We can't have you do that," Frank said, shaking his head. "Michael will do a great job."

"Michael who?" Her tone was a bit snarkier than she wanted.

"Michael Mailloux. I think you went to high school with him."

"Michael Mailloux?" Ally's jaw dropped. "Are you serious?"

"He's really very good," Frank said.

"If you want to learn how to steal kids' lunch money?" It was supposed to be a joke, to break the tension she felt over her fathers choosing a stranger who had been the criminal underboss in high school, but all three looked at her in horror. "What?"

"Someone say my name?"

Ally's heart stopped. Literally stopped beating. She turned around, slowly, hoping that the deep voice behind her wasn't Michael. She looked up to her left and saw a very tall, very handsome man standing in front of her.

Yup, it was Michael Mailloux.

"Hey Ally." He walked past her.

"Hi, Michael." Elise said. "Good to see you."

"You, too." He walked over to Frank and shook his hand, then patted David on the shoulder.

"Today go okay?" David asked, shifting in the hospital bed with a wince. Frank jumped up out of his chair to help. David held up his hand before Frank reached him. "I'm fine."

"Went great." Michael nodded his head. "Tons of business."

"I didn't realize you could bake?" Ally played with the bracelets she'd taken from her dads' place. She didn't mean to sound rude, but she hadn't known. She knew he worked at The Fish Market for her cousin Jack and had for years, but she didn't know he could bake.

"Michael cooked in the military," Frank said, as though being a line cook was equivalent to being a pastry chef.

She remembered how Michael Mailloux had joined the Marines just after they graduated. She thought he had left that same night, didn't even bother showing up to the graduation ceremony.

"Are you able to follow the recipes?" She knew her father's recipe book was incoherent at best. "I can help for the next few weeks, just so you're comfortable with everything."

Michael's face seemed to harden as he stood there silently, not answering her question.

Frank waved his hand at her, as if to fan the idea away. "Oh, we don't want to bother you."

"I can help, it wouldn't be a bother."

"Michael's going to be fine." David's eyes drooped, then slowly began to shut.

Elise stood up and patted Ally's arm. "We should let your dad sleep."

Ally pursed her lips. Frank rushed to her Dad's side, adjusting his blankets as David whispered goodbye to Ally. She looked over to her mom, to Frank, and then to David, trying to catch their eyes, let them in on her anger. But none of them looked at her except Michael, whose stare pierced right through her. If looks could kill, she'd be the one who needed the hospital bed.

But she gave it right back. She could not believe her fathers chose a complete stranger over their own daughter.

"Let's let your dad sleep," Elise said. "You've had such a long day, with all the traveling. You really should take a nap."

CHAPTER 2

"*A*lly!" Her cousin Elizabeth wrapped her arms around her. They stood outside Elizabeth's New England farmhouse in the middle of the driveway. "How are you?"

She pushed Ally out to arm's length to look at her face.

"I'm okay." Ally looked back at her cousin. Always tall and lanky, she had bloomed into radiance with pregnancy. Even with her cantaloupe-sized ankles she looked perfectly adorable. "How are you?"

"The summer's been a bit warm." Elizabeth rubbed her big belly. "How's David?"

"He's okay."

Elizabeth nodded and wobbled off toward the house, hooking her arm into the crook of Ally's elbow. Their friendship never diminished, even after all the time apart.

With the time difference and the stress of David's condition, she did end up taking that nap her mom suggested. Now she was in a funk after waking up. Emotions kept washing up, floating to the surface, a different emotion with each wave. One minute she was grateful her dad had survived such a massive heart attack. The next, she wanted to strangle him for once again leaving her out of being part of any family decision.

"Well, let's eat." Elizabeth opened the door and walked her inside the house. An aroma swept up to greet them, making her stomach growl. She realized she hadn't really eaten at all since she left Paris.

"Lu, she's here!" Elizabeth called out as they walked into the kitchen.

Adam, Elizabeth's husband, stood behind the counter in a chef's apron. He walked over and hugged her. "How was your flight?"

"Crazy, but fine."

The pounding of footsteps was followed by the clatter of dogs running down a wooden staircase. "Bonjour, Tante Ally!"

"Bonjour, ma belle niece, Lucy!"

Ally had expected to see the familiar pig-tailed little girl, but as her cousin's daughter rounded the staircase, she saw not a girl, but a young lady. She had changed so much in just a few months. Her hair was styled. Her cheeks had thinned out, her cheekbones seemed higher.

Ally looked around the farmhouse. She couldn't say she was jealous, because she was happy for Elizabeth. There was no better person than her cousin, and she absolutely deserved true happiness. She had everything she had ever wanted and that was wonderful, it really was, but Ally suddenly felt very alone.

Elizabeth and Ally had been best friends, always. They had been in the same classes through the years, even graduating with the same GPA since they studied together. Elizabeth was the only thing about Camden Cove she missed, having a best friend right down the road. The ketchup to her mustard. Inseparable. People thought they were siblings, and the same last names didn't help. Elizabeth knew all of Ally's secrets and Ally thought she knew hers, but as she watched Elizabeth in her new home, with her new family, Ally had never felt their relationship so unbalanced.

But when dinner was over and Adam brought Lucy to bed, the two sat outside together on the deck. Ally's feelings drifted away as soon as they started talking. It felt good to talk to someone who understood.

"I'm so glad you're back, I just wish it was under different circumstances." Elizabeth gave Ally a sly eye. "Like a wedding?"

Ally gave her a look back. "Umm, no."

"I thought you and Jean-Paul were really good," Elizabeth fished.

"We are. We're just not jumping into anything."

"I know you. You've wanted that diamond since you were in fifth grade with Jake Ryan."

"We've got so much going on. An engagement would just throw everything off." Ally didn't understand why she was lying to Elizabeth. Usually she wouldn't hold back, but she somehow felt different about sharing with someone who had her own Prince Charming locked in a farmhouse with modern amenities. "The patisserie is so busy, and we're just swamped with work."

This was true, and the excuse Jean-Paul gave her every time she mentioned the idea of an engagement.

Elizabeth eyed her again. It was time to change the subject.

"Did you hear about how Frank hired Michael Mailloux as the chef while my dad's recuperating?"

Elizabeth nodded. "Yeah, he's been working for Jack for a while now, ever since he got back from Afghanistan."

"I can't believe they'd hire him."

"Why?" Elizabeth lifted an eyebrow.

"Um, because he's Michael Mailloux." Her anger warmed her chest.

"He's not the same kid he was in high school." Elizabeth poured a glass of wine and passed it over to Ally. "He's a really great guy, actually. Plus, I thought you two seemed to like each other, at my wedding."

"Wasn't he the kid who got caught stealing people's lunches?"

"Ally!" Elizabeth made a face. "That was in middle school."

"Yeah, but still."

"I'd think you'd be grateful, since he's helping out your dads."

Ally bit her tongue before she said anything else. She had expected this conversation to go differently. She'd expected Elizabeth to rally to her, angry about the situation just like she was. Instead, Elizabeth acted like the rest of them, as though Ally was just a visitor who didn't know better.

She looked at her watch and feigned a yawn. "You know, I should get going."

Elizabeth's forehead creased. "Really?"

"Yeah, the flight, you know." Ally stretched for dramatic effect. "I'm exhausted."

"Okay." Elizabeth stood up. "But how long are you staying in town?"

Ally shrugged. "Well, since no one needs me, I think I'll head back soon."

Elizabeth tilted her head, looking Ally over. "They *do* need you, Ally, but they don't want to bother you."

Ally gave a fake smile. "Okay."

"Ally." Elizabeth reached for Ally's hand, but she got up before she could make contact. "They do."

"I think I'll stay for a week, maybe." She ended the conversation. "Jean-Paul's going to need me back soon."

"The Princess is back." Michael walked over to the bookstore counter and set down the books in his hands.

"The Princess?" Harry Weismann, owner of Mainely Murders, looked at his friend. "Like Kate or Meghan?"

"Like Ally Williams."

Harry made a face. "Isn't she nice, now?"

"No, she's anything but nice. She's just like she was back in high school." Michael pulled out his wallet as Harry rang the books up. "She flew in from Paris last night. She started getting on my case at the hospital."

"How's David doing?" Harry asked.

"Fine." Michael went right back to Ally. "She didn't even thank me for helping her father, who had just had a heart attack."

"You seemed to like her at the wedding." Harry bagged up the books and handed them over. "You two seemed to be getting along pretty well if I remember correctly."

"I'm not sure she even remembers the wedding." That fact made Michael even more upset about the encounter with the Ice Princess. She had been completely out of line. Frank had tried to apologize, saying it was because she was so upset about David, but she had been more than rude. It wasn't high school anymore. Had she known why he stole lunches all those years ago, then maybe she'd understand. How many days did *she* have to go hungry as a kid?

Ally Williams had been a rich, stuck-up snob. And clearly, she'd never grown up.

"At least she doesn't live here anymore," Harry countered. "Hopefully you won't have to deal with her much."

"I have a bad feeling this is only the beginning." Michael thought back to Elizabeth Williams' wedding. Ally had been a completely different woman that night. He had actually been looking forward to seeing her. Then he really thought about that night. She had more than a few drinks, was at a wedding in a beautiful restaurant, and she was all alone — the Parisian guy had stayed back home. That bridesmaid dress looked great on her. She looked great. She smelled great. Their kiss was great.

There was no way she'd forgotten that kiss.

Guess he should've put all the pieces together. Ally Williams hadn't changed a bit.

"It's not like we're still in high school." Harry shrugged. "She was probably upset about David's heart attack."

Michael's eyebrows lifted. He looked at his friend in amazement. Harry's status on the social ladder in school had been worse than his. Michael luckily had the strength to knock down anyone who wanted to mess with him. Back then, Harry weighed one-twenty-five soaking wet. He had always been the target, even before Michael started protecting him in grade school. But the guy seemed to have put it all in the past. Must be all the meditating he'd been doing.

"Could you find anything more depressing?" Harry held up William Faulkner's *As I Lay Dying* in his hands.

"It's Faulkner."

"Should I be concerned?" Harry asked.

"I'll see you Saturday, then?" Michael asked, ignoring his friend's razzing.

"I'll be at Sully's after I close at eight." Harry's attention had been stolen by a set of tourists walking into the bookshop.

"Don't forget the dip."

"I know." Harry walked out from behind the counter and up to the group of elderly tourists.

Michael grabbed his books and left his friend's shop. He'd have to call it an early night, with having to wake up at three A.M. to start baking. Ally's voice ground in his head. She hadn't changed since high school. Harry was wrong.

The Princess was back.

Ally walked into the house where Elise and her stepfather Martin lived. The only place she'd ever felt at home. The house had always been beautiful, but casual. Not staged for House Beautiful, like her fathers' place. Elise had all her homeopathic remedies lined up along the counter, with Martin's gadgets scattered everywhere. Ally picked up one of Elise's scarves and nuzzled it to inhale her mother's perfume, Chanel Number Five.

Ally had started to clean up her stuff around the kitchen when Elise walked in.

"Don't worry about it," Elise said. Before Ally left home, Elise would have complained about the mess. Now she was encouraging Ally to leave it. Things really had changed.

"Did you have a nice time with Elizabeth?" she asked, rubbing cream on her hands.

"Yes, it was nice." Ally didn't look at her as she draped the scarf over the back of the kitchen chair.

"It's such a beautiful farm."

"Yes, it's perfect for Elizabeth." Ally sat down. Her cheeks and shoulders were still warm from sitting in the evening sun.

"Would you like to have a cup of tea with me?" Elise asked.

Ally shook her head. She had lost it on the way home, and didn't want to start crying all over again.

"You sure?"

She nodded, then sniffled. "It's been a long day."

"You should go upstairs and get some—"

"—sleep," Ally said.

Elise walked over to her and rubbed her shoulder. "You look miserable."

"Gee, thanks," she grumbled.

"That's not what I meant. It's been a long couple of days for all of us."

"Where's Martin?" Ally asked, looking around the kitchen.

"Upstairs, asleep." Elise grabbed two tea bags and filled the kettle with water.

Ally nodded, but stayed quiet.

"Did you see the new clinic Elizabeth's building?"

"Hard to miss." Ally's voice had an edge.

"And the work they did on the barn?"

Ally could tell Elise couldn't be happier for her goddaughter. "That Lucy is quite something."

Ally rubbed the scarf between her fingers. It must've come from Paris. Camden Cove certainly didn't have scarves like that.

"Did you want to leave Paris when Dad left you?" Ally asked Elise out of the blue.

Elise looked surprised, and shut the water off before answering. "No, but things had changed, and I had you. You were so young at the time."

18

"When did you know about Frank?"

"Really, Ally?" Elise turned the burner on. The clicking of the gas ring crackled through the kitchen. "We're going to have this conversation tonight?"

Ally didn't care if she was pushing her mother's own ignition switch. She wanted to know. "When did you know they were having an affair?"

Elise let out a deep breath and took a seat next to Ally at the island. "Well, I never really knew until they told me they were in love with each other."

"How did you not see it?" Would Ally not be able to tell if Jean-Paul had another woman?

Elise shrugged. "I didn't want to see."

Ally knew she was lucky. Her parents' divorce was as amicable as you could get, but Ally remembered life before the divorce, living in Paris, when Elise first met Frank.

"Wasn't he *your* friend?" She couldn't understand how her mother was still close with Frank to this day.

"Yes, well, things were a bit complicated."

She didn't remember a time without Frank. Her mother had met him at the market down the street from where they lived. He had been an expat like them, but from Canada (which meant he was friendly) and spoke French (he was from Quebec). He worked in the hotel industry and they all became like a little family. They spent all the holidays together, celebrating the Canadian Thanksgiving in October, the American in November. They attended Christmas Eve Mass in a tiny little church, celebrating into the morning with Santa, and New Year's in their apartment. Those were some of the best times of her life. "I would think you'd notice something between the two of them."

Elise tapped her nails against the counter. "Looking back, there were signs. A lot of them, but I didn't want to see them."

"How could you stay friends with Frank after what he did?"

"It wasn't easy." Her mother shrugged. "But we had you to

think about, and well, I didn't want to spend the rest of my life angry."

Ally remembered that her mother's parents were horrified when the marriage ended the way that it did. They didn't know what to think when David and Frank bought the bakery and moved back into town. Her grandfather never forgave David until the day he died, and her grandmother only became slightly less stand-offish at family functions. They all tried to pretend nothing bothered them, like true New Englanders. But Ally felt it.

"The truth is that it might have been Frank who had the affair with David, but it would've been someone else if Frank hadn't been there. Our marriage was far from perfect." Elise walked to the stove when the kettle screamed. "You just don't remember."

"I guess I don't." Ally only remembered the times that were good. She never remembered her parents fighting, never a cross word spoken between the two. When it was just the three of them, Ally felt that life had been perfect.

The chiming of the grandfather clock brought her thoughts back to the present, and exhaustion set in. Maybe she should just go to bed instead of rehashing their lives.

"I just can't believe they hired Michael Mailloux for the bakery."

"I don't know why you're so upset about this." Elise pulled two mugs from the cupboard as the kettle ticked and steam rose from the spout. "He has experience, and Jack said he could work there as long as Frank and your dad need him. If anything, you owe him an apology."

"What?" Ally's mouth dropped open.

"What you said was uncalled for. I was embarrassed. I hoped you would apologize right then, but when you didn't… that's why I said we should leave."

Ally couldn't believe her mother. "He did a lot of bad things in high school."

"Allison Sarah Williams, you of all people should know how bad it is to be judged by everyone." Elise gave her a hard stare.

Ally's eyes brimmed with tears and one slipped out before she could catch it.

"Ally, your dad is going to be okay." Elise placed her hand on Ally's back.

"I just need some sleep." She jumped off the stool and walked out of the kitchen without looking back, muffling her cries with the silk scarf.

CHAPTER 3

$\mathcal{A}$lly rummaged through the drawers of the bakery kitchen, looking for the measuring cups. Everything about her father's kitchen was immaculate, but everything had its own order. David's order. He prided himself on his organizational skills, but nothing seemed to be where it should be. She came down to the bakery when she couldn't sleep. It was morning in Paris. She'd be baking by now.

She noticed a motorcycle pulling up in back as she started turning on the ovens. Elise had gotten to her. She didn't want to apologize, but there she was in the kitchen, pretending to be there to help.

Michael walked in with the same piercing look as he did the other day. He hated her. "What are you doing here?"

"I came to help." Ally closed the drawer, forgetting what she was looking for.

Michael's presence was intimidating at best. Even through his chef's jacket she could see the definition of his muscular chest, reminding her of every Fabio cover in her Grammy Grace's dirty bookshelf by her bed. She adjusted her own jacket, pulling her shoulders back.

"I'm good." He set a book on the counter then stiffed-armed

the door, making it bounce against the wall and stalked out of the kitchen. She peeked at the cover. Faulkner. Ugh. She had read that in high school and hated it.

She took a deep breath and walked out onto the floor. He flipped the coffee machine's switch, ignoring her presence as he turned the lights on in the displays.

"I'm sorry I said what I did at the hospital."

From underneath the counter, he plopped a stack of paper cups next to the register, passing her making her hair blow off her shoulder. "Okay."

Well, he's obviously still in a bit of a huff. "I can help."

"I don't need help from you." He shot her a hard look before bouncing the door off his back returning to the kitchen.

She stood there, unsure what to do next. Who did this guy think he was, anyways? This was her father's bakery. She was a pastry chef at one of the most distinguished patisseries in all of Paris. Thousands, from all over the world, flocked to their doors to taste the marvels they created. She'd had to climb and scratch and claw her way to where she was in her career. He was lucky to have her help. Maybe he'd learn a thing or two from her. Or maybe GI Joe didn't like having a woman teach him things in the kitchen. She had seen that scenario play out enough in her short career.

Even Jean-Paul had been blown away by her talent. That was why he'd offered her a job as a pastry chef in La Patisserie Michalak the very night he met her. In fact, a lot of the other chefs had remarked on her talent, saying they were surprised no one had swept her up yet. She was happy working for Jean-Paul at his patisserie, but she enjoyed hearing things like that. Some day she would like to have her own little place.

She took another deep breath, remembering what her mom had said. He was here to help, too. She pushed the door open and he immediately glared at her.

"You're still here?" he practically growled.

"Look, I'm just here to help, I know how my Dad runs a

kitchen." Michael already had half of the pastries pulled out of the refrigerators and into the ovens, seeming to have no trouble finding the utensils and tools.

"I don't need help."

"I could at least start making some of the breads…" His head tilted forward as the crease between his eyebrows creased. "Okay, I guess you don't need my help." She picked up her bag from the counter.

He started whisking cream in a silver bowl. "Nope."

She clasped her hands together, slowly walking backwards, noticing the muscles in his forearms flexing as he stirred faster. His whole arm was covered in a tattoo of roses. She immediately thought about the wedding and how intoxicated she had been that night, with the champagne and his attention. Her cheeks flushed at the memory of it. She pushed through the door without looking back, hoping he couldn't read her mind. She smacked her forehead as she walked to her car.

Ugh, she couldn't believe she did what she did and said what she said. The memories flooded her mind. It had been so romantic. The wedding on the ocean, the vows, the candles, the champagne. Lots and lots of champagne. Romance had radiated through her. His tattoo of climbing roses echoed the romance. She had practically petted it, asking him the meaning behind it.

"It's for my mom."

"Oh, that's soooooo sweet." She instantly flipped his arm, looking at the whole thing, pulling up his sleeve, rubbing his muscles. "You must really love your mom."

"I do."

She had kissed the guy right then and there. The idea of him dedicating his whole left arm to his mother made the already sexy Marine even more captivating. She had practically forgotten about the fight with Jean-Paul back in Paris, until luckily, maid of honor duties pulled her hands off of him.

The rest of the night was a blur. She was pretty sure they danced and maybe even hung out together at the after party. She remembered getting sick after that. She didn't remember how she got home to her Mom's house, except her car was still at Elizabeth's farm the next day.

She shook her head to stop the night's memories from popping up. She checked the time on her phone. Only a little past three, but really nine in the morning in Paris. She'd go back to Elise's, then maybe visit her dad. Then she didn't really know. No one really seemed to need her.

If Michael's pride wasn't so tender, he would've asked Ally to stay. Although it was one of the most pristine kitchens he had ever worked in, David had such a unique organizational system that he was unable to find anything. He spent most of his time looking through the drawers and cabinets to find what he was looking for. Not to mention, he had a feeling that half the recipes Frank had jotted down were missing ingredients and without any exact measurements, rendering most of them useless. The day before, he had told Frank and David all was well, because the guy just had a heart attack, but it was really okay, at best. This was definitely not one of his shining moments.

He shook his head at the thought of asking Ally Williams to come back and help him. He just needed a couple days in David's kitchen, and he'd be fine.

The pastries would be fine.

"This doesn't taste like David's stuff," his buddy Sully said, when he stopped by to see how things were going.

"Well, it's not David's." As tired as he was, Michael didn't have the patience to endure his friend's insults.

"I'm not trying to be a jerk. They're good, they're just different."

"Bad different or just different?"

"Just different." Sully ate the rest of the pastry. "Well… it's like it's missing something."

"Wow, that really helps."

Sully shrugged, his mouth full of powdered sugar.

"Take your pastries and go."

"Ever since Krissy got pregnant, she's been craving David's chocolate croissants. I hope you didn't mess those up." Sully looked worried.

Michael shoved the bag at his friend. "I make amazing chocolate croissants."

"Yes, but are they like David's, is the question."

"Go back to your house, before I stuff those chocolate croissants where chocolate croissants don't shine."

"You wouldn't."

"Say something about my lemon tarte." Michael narrowed his eyes. "I dare you."

Sully fit the whole tarte in his mouth, grabbed the bag of croissants and backed toward the door. "Saturday night, don't forget to bring more of these!" He held up the bag.

Michael shook his head at his friend. He couldn't believe he was going to be a dad. He thought Sully would be one of the last ones to have children, but there he was with one on the way.

The day went by quickly. Once Frank showed up that afternoon, he took off. He needed to check on his mom before she got tired.

He arrived at the nursing home half an hour before visiting hours ended. The ward where she stayed was in the south wing and furthest from the entrance, but he didn't rush. He knew the time spent there didn't mean anything to her. If anything, it gave her anxiety and stress, because he refused to lie to her.

The smell bothered Michael the most about his mother's residence, Majestic Oaks. The moment the sliding glass doors opened an overwhelming odor of disinfectant and mothballs hit him. The nursing home didn't come close to anything majestic. The irony agitated him. He knew his mother deserved better than a county nursing home, but it was all he could afford.

He reached the heavy wooden doors to the Alzheimer's unit.

Each door had a small window and a sign reading, "Don't let the cat out." The sign really referred to the residents themselves.

He took in a deep breath before opening the heavy doors and heading down the fluorescent-lit hallway. Pastel wallpaper covered the walls, with handrails along the sides. Photographs of the residents hung outside each door.

"Evening," greeted Loretta, the head nurse who took extra delight in Michael and his mother, Rose.

"Hi, Loretta," Michael said, "is my mom in her room?"

"No, honey, she's in the rec room with Robert." He followed Loretta to the large open space at the end of the hall. "She had a long night, but she took a nap this afternoon." She pointed to a woman slumped down in a chair next to the window. "She seems to be in good spirits."

Michael approached the woman who used to be his beautiful mother. She had aged so quickly in this place. Barely recognizable. But her appearance wasn't the worst part. He would have to introduce himself to a blank stare.

"Hey, mom." He rubbed the hand resting on the arm of her chair. Her skin felt waxy and loose. Across the small table sat Robert, fast asleep.

Her eyes widened with alarm. He tried again.

"Rose?" He waited to see if her name would awaken something in her head. "It's me, Mikey."

Nothing.

"Your son."

Her eyes, similar to his own, showed no sign of recognition. He kept talking.

"Today, I worked at that bakery I told you about yesterday. You know, the bakery on the corner of Main and Harbor." Michael stopped. A moan floated from the corner of the room. Gerry was a constant moaner. He continued, "David's daughter is home to help, but she's an absolute nightmare."

A smile grew as she leaned forward in her chair. The blanket covering her legs fell. His mother patted his leg. "When are you going to take me home?"

He leaned down and grabbed the blanket, a gift from some women from the church. He repositioned it back on her lap. He had hoped good spirits would lead to lucid conversation, but Loretta had only meant that his mother wasn't angry or crying.

"You are home, Ma," he said sweetly, but fake.

"Do I know you from Chicago?" she asked, her eyes brightening up. She had moved to Camden Cove over forty years ago.

"I'm your son, Michael." He kept his smile.

"I live in Irving Park. It's right outside of Chicago," she said proudly. "Have you ever been there?"

"Yes I have, actually, with you."

His mother leaned back in her chair and tilted her head, narrowing her eyes in confusion. But she soon forgot her confusion and continued talking. "My parents live there. Are you taking me home?" Her eyes filled with moisture, a hope he would soon crush.

"No, I'm not."

Michael waited for the next question. It was a repeat day. A day where she would ask the same few questions until she fell asleep. He always promised himself he would answer with the truth. Unlike most, who would lie to pacify her, but only upset her more in the end.

His mother's eyes clouded over. "Do you live in Chicago?"

Michael shook his head. Despite the large space, the room closed in on him.

Loretta's footsteps squeaked against the floor as she approached.

"Well, aren't you two having fun?" Loretta put her hands on her hips.

His mother looked up. "Did you know I live in Chicago?"

"I did," Loretta said with gusto. "Did I tell you my Aunt Georgia lived in Chicago? And she never entered the state of

Georgia in all her life." Loretta gave Michael a wink. "You staying much longer?"

Michael shook his head.

"Because Rose here is about to take her bath." Loretta patted his mother's hand. "Would you like to say good night to your son, Michael?"

His mother stroked her fingers along the quilt's edge. She placed her hands on her lap and folded them together. "Do I know you?"

∾

Ally sat in David's hospital room in the chair next to his bed. The Red Sox played on the television.

"How are they doing?" she asked. She picked at her French fries, then set her food container from the hospital's cafeteria on the windowsill.

"They're doing great." He looked at her as though he couldn't believe she asked. "When are the Yankees ever good?"

"So, how do you feel?" she asked, finally alone with him.

"Like I had a heart attack."

It was still shocking to see him in his hospital gown and in the bed, tied up to all the tubes and machines.

"You need to slow down."

"You sound like Frank."

"Well, maybe you should hire another chef and not work seven days a week." The man was stubborn beyond belief. "The best patisseries have more than one chef."

"I'm not one of the best?"

She smiled. "Yes, but you can't be the best if you're having heart attacks all the time."

"Touché." He patted the hospital bed with his hands. "How're things with you? Jean-Paul?"

She thought about what she was going to say. When it came

to Jean-Paul, she had to tread lightly with her Dad. "Busy. The kitchen is in full swing, being summer, you know."

Tourism was the bread and butter for her dad's bakery, so he understood how important a season could be. Sure, he could survive during the winter months, but it was the summer tourists that brought the food to the table.

"Good." He turned back to the game. "Wish I could have a beer."

"Frank would kill you."

He nodded. "That's true. Have you talked to Frank since you got home?"

She shook her head. "Not since yesterday, why?"

"No reason, just wondered." He moved his hand across the bed to hers and squeezed it. "I'm glad you came home."

"Me, too."

They both stared at the television as the announcer talked about an out on third.

"I was thinking of heading back next week, maybe Wednesday. Unless of course you need me to help out. Michael may need an extra hand in the kitchen."

David sipped his water, then shook his head. "Michael has Frank and Kate. He'll be just fine."

She kept her focus on the screen, surprised by the colors blurring together as she pushed back her tears. She spoke carefully. "So, you don't need me at all?"

"No, we're good here."

She nodded, but didn't look at him.

"We know you've got your own life."

More like they had theirs.

She didn't stay much longer, her dad got tired, and she needed air. When she got back to town, she headed to the Tavern to meet her cousins, Matt and Lauren. But as she stood on the sidewalk outside, she felt completely out of place. She wished she was three thousand and six hundred miles away. Plus, the glaring problem was that it had been a whole day now, and Jean-Paul hadn't called her.

She pressed his number. The phone rang, but he didn't answer. It went straight to voicemail. She looked at the time. It was eight o'clock, which meant it was one in the morning in Paris. He was definitely asleep. She'd leave a voicemail.

"Hey, Jean-Paul, it's me, just letting you know that I'm not exactly sure when, but I'll probably head back as soon as next week. Maybe, unless of course things change, but I'll let you know." She paused. "I love you."

She hung up. Then her phone began to vibrate. She looked down. Jean-Paul was calling her back. Her heart relaxed.

"Sorry, did I wake you up?"

"Yes," he moaned.

"It's just that you didn't call like you said."

"You just left, let me miss you first." He mumbled something in French. "How is your father?"

She ignored his comment, but she missed him. She wished he had come with her. "He's okay. The surgery went well."

"I miss you, mon amour." He sounded sincere. "Hurry back."

Ally wasn't sure if it was a French guy thing, being pompous and a bit self-centered. But throughout their year and a half relationship, Jean-Paul seemed like he could always walk away, without looking back, like he had before Elizabeth's wedding. No matter what his stake was in the relationship. His passion for things made her even more insecure. One day, he loved something beyond measure, and the next, he despised it. Plus, most of his friends had casual affairs on their girlfriends and wives all the time. He talked openly about how monogamy didn't work. She also knew she wasn't the first woman he had fallen in love with and wasn't sure if she'd be the last.

She was no fool. If she stayed too long in Maine, chances were that Jean-Paul wouldn't miss her long. He was sexy and talented and had money, all the things that Parisian women were looking for in a man. Not to mention, Paris had an abnormally large number of models and fashion designers and artists, all of whom visited his patisserie, drooling over the man and his creations.

She swore that women undressed Jean-Paul as they ate his delicacies. That's why she needed to go home. So when her cousin Matt asked her how long she was staying and she said, "Probably a couple of weeks," she was completely shocked by her own response.

"Don't you need to get back?" Matt asked.

"Jean-Paul understands." She left it at that. Her cousin wasn't known for conversation.

"Where is Jean-Paul?"

"Where's your girlfriend, Kate?"

He nodded his head, a smirk lifting the side of his mouth. "Touché."

"You were starting to act like our parents."

Matt let out a big laugh. "You know you're in trouble when you start acting like Sarah and Frank. Everything going well in Paris?"

Ally had missed her cousin. Matt was a year older than her and Elizabeth. He treated Ally like his sister. He was a bit annoying, bossy at times, and very over-protective.

"Yeah, great actually. The patisserie is just swamped throughout the day. Did I tell you Jean-Paul got covered in the Paris Sunday newspaper? It's the equivalent to the New York Times Sunday paper, there."

"That's great."

"How about you?"

"I finally have my boat fixed, so I've been trying to catch up." Matt spun his beer. Ally remembered her dad telling her about Matt's boat being sunk in the harbor.

"They ever catch who did it?"

"Freddy Harrington."

"What?!" Her poor cousin had gone through a nasty divorce. His ex-wife's new fiancé had no problem making Matt's life miserable. "I can't believe it! Did he really think he could get away with something like that?"

Matt rolled his eyes. "Yes."

"Did he get arrested?"

Matt took another drink and nodded. "Right in front of Justine." He let out a single laugh. "Now he has to pay restitution and has been doing hours of community service. I saw him in the orange vest along Route One the other day."

"So, where is Kate?" Ally had only heard about *the* Kate. She remembered her coming to Camden Cove as a kid, but never really paid much attention. Summer people… well, were just passing through, not worth taking the time to meet, since they only just turned around and left. But she had heard all about the reuniting Christmas that brought Matt and Kate back together from her dads.

"She's gone to bed, because she's working early."

"Oh, that's right. She's working with Michael. I thought she was a graphic designer?"

"She is, actually, her business is going really well right now. Even in Camden Cove, with the tourist season, a lot of shops liked what she did for your dads."

Ally telepathically screamed at Finn, the bartender, who had been behind the same counter for over forty years, to hurry up and bring her drink. "That's great."

"Yeah, she's really doing well."

"So, like…" Ally registered what he was saying. "She's just working at the bakery to help out?"

"Well, yeah." Matt nodded as Finn handed him another beer. "Thanks, man."

"Ugh, a pale ale."

"Oh, so snobbery came over from Paris."

She ignored her cousin's teasing. "So, she's just helping, like, Dad asked *her*?"

Matt nodded. "Well, she wanted to help, and she's worked there before."

Ally picked up the beer and forced down the American home

brew, chugging half of it.

"Thirsty?" Matt gave a nod to her half-empty glass.

"I can't believe they asked her and not their own daughter."

"Huh?" Matt's attention was stolen by the television.

She looked away from Matt as he returned back to the game. Her dads asked a stranger to run the kitchen and then another practical stranger to run the floor. Did they not want her to work there?

Ally pushed the beer away and grabbed her purse off the back of the chair. "Do you mind if I head home? I have a bit of a headache."

Matt's face turned concerned. "Do you want me to drive you?"

She shook her head, making herself smile. "No, I'll be okay. Sorry about leaving. Will you tell Lauren that I'll stop by soon?"

"Okay." Matt stood up as she handed him a twenty, pushing it back. "I got the tab."

"Thanks, Matt." She gave him a hug.

"Don't forget to stop by the bakery and see Kate."

She pointed her finger at him. "Sure. Will do."

CHAPTER 4

$\mathcal{M}$ ichael got to the bakery extra early, in case Ally showed up again unannounced. He wanted to be the one who opened up this time. To his surprise, she didn't make an appearance, which was a good thing, because things were not getting easier for him. It wasn't that he couldn't bake the pastries, it was that he couldn't bake them like David, and the customers took notice. Things tasted good, but definitely different.

Frank had been so out of sorts, he didn't want to bother him about the recipes, and Kate helped behind the counter but didn't have a clue about baking. He hated to admit it, but the only person who'd really know, besides David, was... Ally.

He could feel his jaw tighten at the idea of having to ask her for help.

Luckily, everything else went fine. Michael kept up the pace, prepped for the day ahead, while also being able to help a bit up front. Frank and David had hired plenty of staff to help. But by the end of the day, he was exhausted. The new hours seemed to have taken a toll, and he wondered if he should skip either visiting his mother, or poker night with the guys.

Just as he sat down to rest for a moment, Ally walked in the back door. He immediately jumped out of the chair and back behind the counter. "What are you doing here?"

"How did things go?"

She sounded like a mother hen checking on her chick. This was not his first rodeo and she knew that, which made the question even more irritating. He didn't give her an answer. He contemplated what he would've done to his Marines if they acted this way in his kitchen.

"So, it went well, I take it." Her eyes rolled to the back of her head. She picked up a tarte from a tray and took a bite. He tried not to look at her, praying to God that she didn't have the same reaction as Sully... except she did. He cringed while waiting for her smart remark, but nothing came.

Then he did what he did best, fix the problem by working on a solution.

He went back to prepping for the morning. He studied the pantry, shelves upon shelves of some of the best ingredients this side of the Atlantic. He rubbed his beard as he looked at all the different glass jars and containers. Unfortunately, he couldn't see what was inside. He pulled out the list of ingredients and stood there, looking, searching, trying to figure out where the heck David put everything. He kept rubbing his beard, hoping one of the ingredients would jump out at him.

"Do you need help finding something?" Out of nowhere Ally stood next to him, making him jump.

"No."

She leaned against the doorframe, watching him as he opened a container to look inside, trying to find the powdered cocoa.

"He has a certain system."

"I gathered that."

"Would you like to know that system?" She crossed her arms, her head tilted to the side, her hair dangling along her tan, smooth, shoulder.

"Nope." He twisted off another lid.

The side of her mouth perked. "Well, good luck, then."

He grabbed another container off the shelf, pulling up the lid.

"It's arranged by what he uses most." She let out a huff. "He puts all the ingredients at waist height, so all he has to do is reach out and grab them."

She pointed to the middle shelf, and right before him in a glass jar sat a dark chocolate powder. He let out a chuckle. "That's crazy."

"Tell me about it." She dropped her arms and picked up another jar filled with what he assumed was baking soda, the second ingredient on his list, and handed it over to him. She then pulled out a small rolling cart from the corner.

"Thanks." He set the cocoa and baking soda down.

"Are you sure you don't need help?" This time her voice had lost that aggravating tone.

"Nah, I'm good, now that I have some sort of idea what he's thinking."

She nodded, then stuffed her hands in her pockets. "Are you listening to country music?"

"Yeah? You got a problem with country music?"

She shook her head. "No, it's just not something I ever heard in the bakery before."

"What does David listen to?"

"Bach."

"Oh, hey Ally!" Kate said coming in from the front.

Ally's attention moved to Kate, and Michael gave his full attention to his list. Flour, sugar, fresh eggs. Awfully nice of Kate, who had her own job, to come and help out, when Princess over there just hung around and ordered them around. Was working a counter not good enough for her?

"I'm so glad to help, you know," Kate said, smiling.

Ally was not smiling.

"Well, it's just *so* nice of you." Ally's head tilted again, her hair falling across her smooth shoulders, her tank top clinging perfectly to her back. He shook his head.

"Of course, your dads are like family." Kate laughed a bit

nervously. He wasn't surprised, he could tell that Ally intimidated her. Half of Camden Cove High shook in their boots at the sight of Ally Williams walking their way. She had beauty, a queenly demeanor that intimidated other women, and the confidence that made her absolutely perfect at being a brat.

Every guy wanted her, and every girl wanted to be her.

Michael just wanted her out of the kitchen.

"I heard you're an amazing chef, as well. David says you're even better than him."

"He does?" Ally almost sounded surprised.

"Oh my God, they talk about you all the time," Kate went on. "Do you love Paris?"

"Yes, it's beautiful."

"I've always wanted to go."

"You and Matt should come out during the winter, when he's not fishing. You can find really cheap flights, if you don't mind the cold."

"Paris in winter would be amazing."

Ally smiled. "So, are you sure no one needs my help?"

"I mean, I don't think so…?" Kate looked over to Michael.

Then Ally looked at him. She almost seemed to be begging. "Nah, we're good."

Ally's face changed. "Well, I should go. Good seeing you."

He knew she was only talking to Kate.

"You, too!" Kate gave her a hug.

"I guess I'll go." Ally gave him a quick wave, but she didn't even look to see if he returned the gesture. He probably wouldn't have, even if she did look.

He had to figure out the recipes. He'd have to skip the poker game. A long night was ahead of him.

Ally walked without knowing where she was going until she ended up at the beach. The crowds were dwindling with the late afternoon. Only the true beach goers or the late arrivals still hung around. A few surfers sat on their boards out on the water, but there weren't too many swimmers. The water was hardly over sixty degrees, even if it was late June.

Even though the sun hung low in the sky, the heat still stung her shoulders. She sat there as the waves crashed along the sand, the tide moving in with nowhere to go.

Frank was at the hospital with her dad.

Her mom and Martin had a golf thing.

Elizabeth was with Lucy at riding lessons.

She felt more alone here than she ever did in Paris.

In Paris, she had Jean-Paul and her friends. She had work. She had an apartment on the fifth floor, with a window you could see the cathedral dome from if you stepped on the kitchen chair. She had a city brimming with creativity like a pot of simmering water. Her mind made sense in Paris. Here, no one knew her anymore. They only thought they did.

Kate was more family than she was at this point. The way her dads talked about the newcomer to Camden Cove not only annoyed her, but made her even more mad, because Kate was awesome. She filled the daughter role they had always wanted, to a tee. Ally and her dads always seemed to be clashing. They always seemed to have a bit of apprehension when she was around. No one wanted to step on each other's toes, so no one did anything but tiptoe around each other.

She dug her feet in the sand as she sat on the bench, dried pieces of seaweed scratching against her soles. She did miss the beach. That, Paris didn't have. The sounds, the smells, and the sights only the ocean could deliver. No lights or towers could compete with the edges of the Atlantic.

She thought about the tarte and how pissed she was that it wasn't right. Michael's tarte was not David's tarte. Either he couldn't figure out David's recipes, or he just chose to do his own thing. If she had to guess, it was probably a mixture of both.

He knew she was on to him. That smoldering look he'd given her also, sadly, reminded her of the wedding, which made her instantly hot and uncomfortable, and she'd wanted nothing more than to get out of there. Images of her dirty dancing with him popped into her head. She shook it as if that would wash them away. Would that night ever stop rattling around in her head? She must've been the biggest idiot, ever.

She didn't want to even think about it.

What if he told people about it?

What if he told Kate?

Or worse, Frank?

That would go over well, since her family already thought Jean-Paul was a big mistake.

Sully's wife Krissy, who was eight months pregnant, looked like she was about to pop. She shuffled her feet against the floor as she walked around the kitchen, trying to be the same wife she had been before the pregnancy, just a hundred times slower. Not that Michael was complaining, he couldn't believe how lucky Sully was to have her.

"Hon, go sit, lie down, we're fine." Sully got up, grabbing the trays of food from her hands.

"Sully, this might be one of your last guys' nights before the baby comes, it's not going to be this easy for me in a really long time."

"I know, but we're good, hon. We've done it before we had your help, we can do it again."

Michael shuffled out the cards.

She stood there, tears building up in her eyes. "You're good without me?"

"Ah, hon, no." Sully stood up and chased after his wife as she left the kitchen in tears, leaving Harry and Michael alone.

"So, how's it going at the bakery?" Harry asked, throwing down two cards.

Michael looked at his hand. *Kinda cruddy.* Harry shuffled out three cards. "I can't figure out David's recipes, and Frank's been really upset about everything so I haven't been able to ask him."

He thought about Ally's face at the bakery that afternoon. She had tasted the difference, too, just like Sully, and it pissed him off. He stayed there trying to figure out the secret ingredient David put in his *pain au chocolat*, but he couldn't place it. And that's what separated him from her, and he hated it, his toes curling at the thought. That's what fancy culinary schools got you. Not cooking on the line in the middle of the desert in Afghanistan. But at a posh patisserie where sous chefs did all your prep and dirty work.

Nonetheless, the very idea that Ally baked made her even hotter. A woman kicking butt in a man's world seemed appropriate for her, but also very desirable.

"Why don't you ask Ally, since she's in town?"

"No."

Harry made a face. "So, still not getting along?"

"No, still not getting along." Michael looked at the clock, thinking about getting to the bakery even earlier tomorrow morning.

Harry pushed up his glasses, then took a drink of his coffee. "I'd get over it and ask her."

"No."

"Oh, I see," Harry laughed, shifting in his chair. "You still have a thing for Ally."

"You can't be serious?" he looked at his cards, ignoring Harry.

"Then ask her."

Michael immediately looked up at his friend's dare. This wager was almost too much. He could hardly be in her presence for more than a minute, much less the whole day. Her bossing him around, watching over him. "Heck no."

"You have the hots, face it."

"Do not." Michael grabbed a handful of nuts and popped one in his mouth, so he didn't have to talk.

"Then it shouldn't be a problem asking for her help, now should it?" Harry raised the stakes. The word chicken was on the tip of his tongue.

"What wouldn't be a problem?" Sully asked, walking back into the kitchen.

"Everything okay with Krissy?" Michael tried to change the subject.

"She's watching her show, happy." Sully picked up his cards and threw two down.

"Michael has the hots for Ally Williams again."

"I don't." Michael started arranging his cards, focusing on his hand.

"You mean the Ally who you let rub your tattoo all night?" Sully smirked.

Harry gave Sully a high-five as they laughed at his expense.

"The tattoo is for my mom," Harry said, purposefully lowering his voice to mock him.

"It is." Michael rolled his eyes.

"It goes all the way up my arm," Sully said, also lowering his voice. "Let me show you my biceps."

"Ha ha, very funny." Michael put down his cards and wiped his palms, trying not to give in to those two. "She certainly isn't like the woman she was the night of the wedding." Michael wanted this done. "She's a snob."

"Well, it's not really about you," Sully shrugged. "It's not that your pastries are bad, they're not David's, and you wouldn't want his business to get reviews on Yelp and stuff because of it."

"Gee, thanks." But Michael didn't want that.

"Plus, she could teach you some stuff, which would make you even better," Harry chimed in. "You've always wanted to go back to school. She's got to be really good."

Sully nodded. "She works in a Paris bakery."

Michael bounced his knee, trying to let go of the animosity he had built up inside of him since the scene at the hospital. He'd been at war he could handle a pompous brat.

"Fine, but when I make her cry, and Frank and David fire me, you'll owe me one."

CHAPTER 5

*A*lly's stepfather, Martin, had built their house the winter before he married her mother. It took him nine months to finish the property, one of the few winterized houses on the water. The house hugged the cliffs of the Atlantic Ocean. Too high to get to the water, but too close to escape it. He went through every detail with her mother, trying to please her and Ally both. She had been ten.

Strangely, it was one of the best summers of her life. Martin seemed to understand Ally the most. His naturally quiet manner calmed her every time she was in his presence. He never judged her or her choices, or worried over her. He seemed to have complete faith in her abilities, never once thinking she wouldn't get into the culinary program at Academie Culinaire or the apprenticeship at Les Caprices de Nicolas, or win Pastry Chef of the Year at her school. He always believed she could do it.

Whenever she had something to talk about, she'd sit in his study while he worked on something, and he'd just let her talk it out. Never interrupting or forcing his advice on her, just asking a few questions to make her think, and soon she'd have an answer.

She wished she could sit in Martin's study again and have him guide her through her problems, but she didn't want to disappoint him. Even after all those talks, he hadn't fixed her. She was still the same girl who couldn't get out of her own way.

If she was mature enough, she'd just ask Dad or Frank if she could work, or suck it up and ask why they didn't want her to work at the bakery. If she could grow up, she would have just helped Michael, without being a jerk about it. If she could get over her issues, she wouldn't be jealous of all the people around her. If she was mature enough, she'd let it all go.

But she wasn't, and she couldn't.

So, she knocked on her stepdad's office door. "Hey Martin. Mind if I come in?"

He looked up, peering over the top of his glasses, and smiled. "I was hoping you were going to ask me that."

She smiled in return and looked around the space, the only room without a view of the water in the whole house. She once asked why he didn't give himself the best room. He told her he wanted to give them all to her mother and her.

"How is everything?" he poked at his model car.

All the words were on the tip of her tongue when Elise hurried in. "Martin! Ally! Come see the whales!"

Martin shot up from his chair. A whale sighting or a seal, sometimes certain seagulls they recognized, a boat, a sighting of her cousin Matt, were all events to her mother, and had to be shared.

"Where?"

Elise rushed out onto the back deck. Martin grabbed the binoculars on the table before running out the door. Ally sat down in his office. If she had been transported back fifteen years, this moment would be exactly the same. The same issues, the same dramas. She'd just have to get through this week.

Then her phone rang.

It was Frank.

"Hey Frank," she said. "Is Dad okay?"

"Yes, fine." His voice was soft. "I was hoping you could pick up your dad's computer from the bakery before you come to the hospital this afternoon."

She leaned her head on the back of the chair. She didn't want to see Michael ever again.

"Sure."

"It's a humpback!" she heard Martin exclaim from outside.

Ally would wait to go visit David until the bakery had closed, so she could get in without having to deal with Michael. That was the plan, but when she arrived, Michael stood by the back door, waiting for her. "Seriously?"

"What?"

"Frank told me you were coming about two hours ago."

"I didn't realize I had to pick up the computer within a certain time limit." She walked past him, done with the conversation.

He turned around, her dad's recipe binder in his hands. "Do you know how to read these?"

"Yes." She dragged out the word as a smile grew on her face. Was Mr. Marine going to ask for help? He opened his mouth, then shut it. Then opened it again and said, "I need." He stopped and looked as though he literally had to swallow his pride as he took a big gulp of air. "I need your help reading what your dad wrote."

She pressed her tongue against the inside of her cheek to hold back her smile. "Are you asking for my help?"

"Yes," he said through a clenched jaw.

Maybe now her dads would realize she was the one they should've asked in the first place. "What do you need?"

"What are you doing now?" he asked.

"I'm about to see my dad." She looked over at the computer, then back to him. She wasn't going to let him call the shots, anyways. "I can come tomorrow morning."

"Fine, that would work." He nodded at her.

"At three."

His jaw flexed before he answered, "I'll be there."

When Michael pulled his motorcycle into the back of the bakery the next morning, lights were already on inside. Ally was there before him, and it was two-thirty A.M. No one else in the whole town of Camden Cove was up besides the two of them. She looked out the back windows as he came inside.

"Good morning," he said, taking out his notebook and apron from his backpack. He had decided last night to let it all go and start fresh, like Harry suggested.

"Good morning." Ally had her hair up in a bun, but wore a scarf around her head. She wiped away the wisps of hair that dangled out of the scarf with her forearm. "I figured I'd just prep a few things while I was here."

Michael looked around the kitchen. All of the clean surfaces he'd left last night had been smeared and daubed with various ingredients. Cream had spilled on the stove, granular sugar glistened on the countertops, and his shoes slipped in flour on the floor. "How long have you been here?"

"All night." She threw down a ball of dough onto the marble countertop. She kneaded it, rolling her palms out. Her hands looked dainty inside the big dough ball, yet she handled it with almost no thought, sprinkling on the flour when needed, rolling it out, pulling it, and slapping it.

He became instantly annoyed. "I thought you were going to help me figure out your dad's recipes, not bake them for me."

"I am."

"This isn't helping me." He flung his hands at all the prepped food. Then he marched across the room, hitting the swinging door, knowing what he was about to see. The shelves were already stocked with every pastry David made. "You made everything already?!"

"You're welcome."

"How is this helpful?"

"Are you seriously upset right now?"

The snotty tone in her voice curled his toes. He pulled his apron off over his head and grabbed his backpack. "So, you're sticking around then?"

"What?"

"You're going to stick around for a few months when your dad's in recovery?" He unzipped his bag, stuffing the apron inside.

"What's happening here?" Her hands went directly to her hips.

"You're going to stay, and not go back to your home in Paris?"

"Well, I—" She started to talk, but he interrupted her.

"Because if you weren't staying until David's completely better, especially during the busiest season of all, then you'd be doing whatever it took to help out, right? Like going through some of the recipes, or oh, I don't know, making sure the person who *could* stay, doesn't quit."

"I cannot believe you're upset right now." She crossed her arms over her chest. "I'm sorry I baked?"

"Everything!" He flung his hands out. "You baked everything!" She didn't get it. Now she was giving him the crazy look, like he was losing it. "Did you want to prove that you can bake, or something?"

"No." She looked insulted.

"Then you're going to show me all those recipes right now, since you're the one who made me come in this early."

"I planned on it."

"What?"

"I just prepped the front, so we could have the whole morning to go through everything." She shook her head. "My goodness, you get in a tizzy."

Michael cocked his head toward her, confused. "You're going to show me?"

"Yes, but I figured it'd be easier if we didn't have to worry about making everything. Now we can take our time to rewrite the recipes." She held up a computer. "On David's computer."

He stood, frozen with his backpack, suddenly feeling absolutely ridiculous. The kitchen grew warmer with every passing second. "I'm sorry. I thought…"

"Huh?" Her voice was sarcastic. She went back to kneading the dough. "What was that?"

He might be wrong, but that didn't change what he thought of her, which was that she was a complete princess, who had no idea what it was like for the other ninety-nine percent. Even if she looked hot twisting the dough. "I'm sorry."

She pulled the bowl on the counter closer to her and plopped the dough inside, covering the top with plastic and sticking it in the fridge.

"We'll start with Madeleines and tartes, and move through his menu." Ally wiped her hands on her apron. Then she moved past him and turned on the pantry light. "I also rearranged the pantry to be more like a real kitchen."

Michael peeked inside and couldn't believe it. She might be a mess while she baked, but the pantry was beautiful. Everything put in an order that made sense, with tags hanging from the metal shelving. "Thank you."

"Should we start?"

When she walked back to the counter, passing by him, he smelled a perfume he'd known his whole life. The same perfume his mother had put on for special occasions. Chanel Number something…? Memories flashed through his head.

Huh.

He hadn't thought of those memories in years. A time when his mother was happy.

Ally opened up the computer. "I'll type everything out, so you can have an accurate recipe."

Michael stood there watching as she typed. Harry might be right after all. Maybe she wasn't so bad.

"So, how much do you know?" her voice was condescending.

Maybe Harry was wrong.

He stared at her without answering.

She rolled her eyes. "I mean, what pastries would you like to focus on?"

"I can bake your typical dessert." Michael couldn't believe he had to do this. "I just need help with some of the fine tuning."

Ally nodded and pulled out the sugar and the eggs, then stood there. "So?"

"What?"

"You going to put down that bag, and fine tune?"

He looked down at the backpack still in his hands. He unzipped it and pulled out his apron. "What's first?"

He threw the bag on the bench against the wall and tied the apron behind his back.

"We'll cream together the eggs and sugar, and while that's happening, we'll grind up some vanilla beans."

"No extract?"

"You found extract?" She shook her head. "Never use extract."

So, there's one mistake, he thought to himself. He should've pasted the beans the other day. Ally took a few vanilla beans, opening them up with a knife and scraped out the seeds from the interior. The scream from the motor filled the quiet as he cracked the eggs into the mixer and poured in the sugar. He slipped the switch onto high speed, watching it for a minute before turning back to find her staring at him.

"What?"

"I didn't know you baked."

"That surprises you?" He rested his hand on top of the mixer, watching the whisk on the mixer spin madly around.

"Yes."

He looked at her, surprised by her honesty for some reason, even though most people were surprised when they heard that he liked baking.

"You're just this Marine guy, that's all."

"It's where I learned how to bake."

She raised her eyebrows with curiosity. "Really?"

"I enjoyed trying to bake something out of our limited

supplies in the field. Something good to give the guys, once in a while."

"I do prefer the simple recipes, like this madeleine, where you can taste the flavors of all the ingredients." Ally put the paste into a jar then grabbed a measuring spoon. "If you're using paste, it's half a teaspoon." She handed over the leveled spoonful, then pulled out a measuring cup and filled it with flour. "After the dry ingredients, we'll let it sit for an hour in the fridge before adding the butter and honey."

She got everything else ready, then moved to the computer and typed.

For the rest of the early morning, before everyone showed up to open, she walked him through half a dozen of David's recipes, explaining each step as they went along. The princess routine had completely vanished. If anything, Michael could feel her passion for everything she was doing. She made the act of baking an art form. The way she whisked, added ingredients, when she cut corners and when she took her time. By the time Frank showed up, he stood in the kitchen, stunned. "Ally, what are you doing here?"

"Michael asked me to help," she said. She clearly ignored the surprised look on Frank's face. He couldn't figure out if Frank was happy about it or not, and he was pretty sure Ally couldn't figure it out either. "Is that a problem?"

"No, of course not." Frank smiled, but his exhaustion came out in the dark circles under his eyes. "I just wasn't expecting you."

Kate arrived later in the morning and by then, Ally and Michael had gone through most of the menu. Although he had started deciphering some of Frank's notes, he appreciated Ally going through each recipe.

"You should run his cooking classes," he said to her, remembering a side conversation at the hospital between David and Frank. "They were going to cancel them, but you're really good."

Ally took a tray of eclairs out of the oven. "I've never taught before."

"You're teaching me." Michael looked up from the computer. "You have all the recipes. People would eat the 'Parisian patisserie chef' thing up."

"Yes, well, you clearly already know your way around a kitchen."

Frank came in, and before Michael thought about it, he said, "You haven't canceled the cooking classes this week, yet, have you?"

Ally whipped her head around at him, her mouth dropping open.

"The classes!" Frank slapped his forehead with his hand. "I forgot about the classes again." He leaned against the counter. "Your dad is going to kill me."

"I can do them."

He smiled to himself as Ally took his dare.

"Oh, I couldn't ask you to do that." Frank shook his head. "No, I'll just cancel them."

Instantly, Ally's face deflated. Her shoulders slowly slumped forward, and then with a nod, she said, "Sure, no, that makes sense."

"Ally would be great," Michael shot out. He examined Frank, trying to figure out his hesitation.

"I'd just hate to take up more of your time."

"I'm here for couple of weeks at least," she said. "I could take the next few classes so you're not canceling everything."

Frank nodded. "That would be really great. Are you sure you don't mind?"

Ally stood up straighter. "Not at all."

Frank smiled. "I'm taking your dad home tonight. I'm thinking of giving him a quiet night, but we would love to have you for dinner tomorrow?"

Ally nodded. "Sure."

"Are you sure you don't mind taking on the classes?" Frank asked.

Ally looked around and lifted her hands. "Nope, I'd love to help."

"I'm just going to finish a few things up front."

From Michael's perspective, Frank looked as though he didn't want to impose more on Ally, but as Ally pounded the bread dough, he could tell she didn't see it that way.

"So, you and him seem to mesh well."

"Yeah, we're real bosom buddies."

"Hmmm."

"I know what you're going to say, something must be wrong with me." Her voice sounded defensive. "Frank's the nicest guy in the world."

"I didn't say that."

She slapped her hand to her chest. "I'm the difficult one."

Michael didn't say anything, because he could tell she was going to keep going.

"But he avoids me."

Michael thought about it. Frank *had* been up front the whole day, but that's where he worked, so it made sense.

She looked away, her eyes catching the other side of the bakery. "People I don't even know will tell me he's like family to them, but with me... he's different."

Michael rolled his eyes. "Oh, save me the pity party."

She whipped back toward him. "Excuse me?"

"I mean, he's just scared." Michael shrugged.

"He's scared of me?"

"Scared of bothering you."

"If that's what you call it."

"What do you think?"

"I think he still thinks of me as the same teenage girl I was before I left." Ally went from one pastry puff to the next. "Everyone still thinks I'm that girl."

"Everyone sees you as our precious homecoming queen."

"Ugh, that's exactly my point." Ally shook her head. "I can't wait to leave."

She picked up the piping bag and began filling the center of the puff pastry with vigor.

"Like you had it tough in this town," he murmured.

"Are you kidding me?" She over-filled a puff, white crème squirting everywhere. "Having your dad married to a guy was not exactly easy in this little town."

"At least you *had* a dad or two," Michael murmured.

She looked as though she was about to argue, but shut her mouth. She must have remembered his story.

"Maybe you should talk to him instead of destroying my pastry puffs." He nodded at the dough squeezed between her fingers. She looked down, and dropped the mess on the counter.

"Sorry." She took a seat on the stool. "I don't mean to compare families."

He shrugged, thinking about his. He thought about his mom, wondered where in the rec room she'd be sitting. He hadn't even seen his dad since he was a kid. He had no siblings. He'd kill for a family. "You all just have a misunderstanding."

"This is more to me than a misunderstanding." She shook her head. "This is how our relationship has always been, strangely distant."

"I think he doesn't want to get in the way of your big fancy life." Michael opened the oven and slid a sheet pan of turnovers inside, set the timer and shut the door. "They just want to make you happy."

She covered the puffs with cellophane. "I know, but they don't ask me if I am or not."

"Well, Princess, only you can make yourself happy."

Ally knew it wasn't her dads' job to make her happy, but she wanted to be at least considered part of the family. Frank hadn't even called her about the heart attack until after the surgery. He didn't want to "interrupt" her at work. The whole town of Camden Cove, however, probably all stood inside the hospital waiting room as it happened.

Now, even though she thought La Patisserie Michalak was where she had been most happy, she found the idea of going back less and less appealing. She enjoyed running the kitchen this morning on her own, making what she wanted, how she wanted, what she thought tasted best with the ingredients she thought went best together. She enjoyed the quiet rhythm and solace a small kitchen could provide. She hadn't really baked like that in years. At La Patisserie Michalak, she managed the tarte station, and mostly Jean-Paul's ego. The patisserie had so much business and so many customers throughout the day, she had to push the pastries out, and fast. Never did she get to change the recipe without a huge discussion and a huge consideration on Jean-Paul's part. Never did she get out on the floor and meet the customers. She really didn't miss that part at all.

She didn't really want to admit how much more she enjoyed working in the kitchen with Michael. She enjoyed showing him some of the things she had learned over the years, and he actually respected her baking. He also wasn't afraid to spin it his way, but not to upstage her or prove his worth. He was a pastry chef at heart. He may not have been taught by a master baker, but what he had taught himself was impressive.

What she liked most about being at the bakery was that she realized she still had the fire inside her that she thought had burnt out. And the fire grew when she heard compliments from the customers, grew more when she experimented with ingredients, or saw what else she could do. The possibilities were endless.

She didn't miss La Patisserie Michalak, but she did miss Jean-Paul.

And Jean-Paul hadn't called. It had been only a few days, but still, he hadn't called her. He didn't miss her, in other words. His sarcastic remark seemed more like teasing when he first said it, but now she wasn't sure if he was *ever* going to miss her.

"So, David must've taught you everything, huh?" Michael asked, as they finished the last of the breads.

She shrugged. "Sort of. When I was little, he'd teach me stuff, but then, I'd play with stuff on my own."

"Your *pain au raisins* and *palmiers* are delicious." He bit into the palmier puff pastry.

She looked around to see if anyone else had heard, and smiled. "Yes, well, it's all about the ingredients. Fresh butter, eggs from the farm, and cream always makes it taste better."

"Thanks again for helping." He handed the baking sheet to the kid whose lucky job of washing the dishes kept him busy all day. She wasn't sure, because he faced away from her, but she thought she saw him smile.

After closing, she finished typing up the last of the recipes for the immediate menu, but she figured she'd come back and show him the more specialized desserts David did by special order, and for weddings. The wedding cakes, the pastry bar he offered with all the different finger treats. That was another few days, at least.

"I can come—"

"Could you come?"

"You first," Michael said.

"I was about to say I could come in for the next couple of days to help." She swiped her hair away from her face. "But if you don't need me…"

"No, that'd be great."

She nodded. Suddenly the exhaustion of staying up all night hit her like a ton of bricks and she yawned, loud and long and hard.

"Go home," Michael said. "I've got it from here."

"No." She yawned again. "I can help."

"Tomorrow would be great."

Kate walked into the kitchen, bringing in more empty trays. "We got so many compliments today!"

Ally grabbed the trays out of her hands. "That's great."

"They loved all of it."

Frank swung the kitchen door open and removed his apron. He looked as tired as she felt. "Well, I have to say, everything went perfectly today."

"It was Ally who baked today."

"Michael helped with everything."

"Only with the afternoon rush."

"Well, I can't thank you both enough." Frank sat on the bench and slumped against the wall. "I think I'll go to the hospital and bring your dad home, now."

"I can come and help bring him home?" Ally asked.

Frank lifted his head. "No, I can do it."

CHAPTER 6

The following days were unusually warm, and even along the Atlantic Ocean, there was no breeze. The kind of day Michael enjoyed most. He sat on the bench facing the harbor outside the bakery as he took his break. He grabbed a few of Ally's *craquelines*. a French pastry he had never even heard of. It was made from brioche dough with candied orange slices inside, toasted almond slices and a sugary syrup on top.

He'd taken so many notes over the past few days that he bought a new notebook and rewrote them all over again, then into a computer file. He took notes on the recipes themselves, but also what she did. How she whisked some ingredients by hand rather than using the mixer, or how she preferred a buttered metal pan for her loaf cakes versus a silicon one, or how she drizzled syrup on her cakes the moment they come out of the oven. Most of the recipes she knew off the top of her head, and as she went through the motions, she'd explain everything.

She went by equations. Her pie crust was a 3-2-1 ratio of flour, fat and liquid, whereas a *pate au choux* pastry dough had a 1-1-2-2 ratio, flour, fat, liquid and egg. She did most of her measurements by weight instead of volume, something he'd never done before.

She threw cocoa powder instead of flour on the counter to keep the chocolate doughs and batters from sticking, and used milk powder to add richness and help with the browning.

Everything she did, she explained. Michael had learned more in the past few days with Ally than he had in the last ten years of cooking. Something about the way she understood every single detail of creating the pastry was… well… sexy.

"Whatcha reading?" Without warning, Ally stood in front of him, blocking the sun, so it made it hard to see her face.

He turned the book to its cover.

She read the title out loud in a disapproving tone. "For Whom the Bell Tolls?"

He looked back at the cover. "Some might say this is Hemingway's greatest work."

"Ugh." She shook her head. "Maybe you should switch off and do some light reading, like Voltaire or Dostoyevsky?" She giggled at her own joke.

He crossed his leg as he took a bite of her pastry, looking up at her darkened face. "I thought I was on break?"

"Oh, I figured I'd bother you while you read, and take a break at the same time, since the front is covered." She pulled out a salad in a plastic container.

"Are you kidding me?"

"What?"

"You're eating a salad for breakfast?"

She took out a swig from her water bottle before answering. "What's wrong with having a salad?"

"It just doesn't taste as good as your pastries."

She smiled, then poked her fork into the greens. "Well, if I ate all I baked, I'd have a heart attack like my Dad."

"Touché."

She rolled her eyes. He had found a way to use French phrases throughout the day, purposely trying to annoy her.

"Besides, salad can be delicious."

"Not at nine in the morning." He held up the last bite of craquiline. "And not better than this."

She crunched the lettuce and nodded. "The craquilines did come out pretty good."

He had been surprised by how humble Ally was about her baking. She wasn't humble about much, except her gift. And she had talent, the kind of talent that would get swooped up by the big restaurants and bakeries in the city. She could work anywhere. What surprised him more, from what she had told him, was that she was basically an assistant chef. She should be running her own bakery, not running errands for another baker.

"I'm going see my dad after the lunch crowd, then I'll have time to prep for the class tonight, thanks to you." She moaned.

"You'll be great at bossing everyone around." He smirked.

"Ha, ha."

She had brought up the class a few other times that morning and he could tell she was nervous, even though he didn't understand why. "What if I helped?"

"Like how?"

He shrugged, swallowing the last bite of pastry. "I could be the assistant, making sure everyone's following along and stuff."

She thought about it for a moment. "Alright, but only if you wear that apron you did the other day."

"You mean my Marine apron?"

"Yes, the one with the camouflage." She winked. "Semper fi."

"Oorah."

She laughed. "It'll keep the Golden Girls at bay."

"Golden Girls?"

"Have you seen the crowd that takes David's cooking classes?"

Michael had no idea who would take the classes, but when it started that night and he stood behind the crowd of mostly gray-haired women, Ally mouthed the words, *I told you so* from the other side of the kitchen. He laughed to himself, looking out at the silver heads.

"Okay, ladies and gentlemen, welcome to La Patisserie's introductory course to making the most delicious and popular pastry in all of France, the pain au chocolat."

Ally opened a silver cake stand cover, revealing dozens of croissants oozing with chocolate piled into a pyramid shape. The men and women whispered to themselves behind their rolling tables. Michael had already placed most of the ingredients into glass bowls to make things easy on them.

"We're going to go step by step, and by the end, you'll be able to take home a baker's dozen of these delicious pastries."

~

Ally's stomach cramped with anxiety as she walked around each table, moving between groups. Michael helped a couple who were confused about how to use the scale. Most of the others seemed to be doing okay. A few questions, but mostly they all seemed to be enjoying themselves.

Two women near the front had clearly done some baking and were ahead of the class, giggling as they drank their wine.

"You do a marvelous job of teaching us old folks," the first woman teased.

"We were so sorry to hear about David," the other woman said.

"Yes, please tell him we're thinking of him and that we'll see him next year," the first woman said.

"Thank you, I will." Ally nodded and moved to the next table. She thought about David's reaction when she told him she'd do the classes. He looked relieved, compared to Frank's worry.

Another couple looked like they were having trouble folding the croissant over the chocolate ganache. Michael showed the man how to hold the dough, sprinkling a bit of flour to make it less sticky from the summer heat crawling into the air-conditioned kitchen. She watched as Mr. Marine delicately folded the pastry over the chocolate. His arms bulged as he daintily handled the pastry dough. There was something about his hands that she couldn't resist studying. They looked solid, strong, like he could crush someone with them, yet performed some of the most technical steps in baking. She wanted to reach out and touch them.

What was that about?

Once the pastries were in the oven, she set out the leftover goodies from the day with coffee and tea. The group mingled, talking about their stay in the small community, the restaurants they'd eaten at, and the hotels where they were staying. The energy in the room was contagious. Even Michael seemed to have a smile on his face instead of his usual scowl.

Ally recommended a few quaint places to shop and eat off the main strip, a bit further out of town. They all asked about her culinary background. Paris came up every time someone asked a new question. She enjoyed talking about her time in the City of Light. She lived in the 18th arrondissement, in the quaint Montmartre. She gave Jean-Paul's patisserie name. A woman googled and showed the photograph of the bakery. Ally couldn't connect to that picture now that she was looking in from the outside. The pristine showroom looked more like a boutique than a bakery.

As she looked over the group, she saw Michael watching her. When he noticed her attention, he gave her a smile and she smiled back. Maybe Mr. Marine wasn't such a jerk.

Soon, the pastries had turned a perfect golden brown, with chocolate oozing through the sides.

"They look beautiful," someone said, as Ally took the first set of thirteen from the oven.

Michael helped her box everyone's pains au chocolat along with a flyer featuring upcoming events. Some finished their wine with the warm chocolate pastries at their table, while others decided to take them to the outdoor tables to watch the sunset behind the harbor.

"This was fabulous," a couple said on their way out. "Good luck in Paris!"

"Thank you!" Ally wanted to reach out and hug them all. She'd make sure to do another class before she left.

As the last of them exited, Michael filled a bucket of hot water and soap and started washing the tables as she swept.

"This was a lot of fun, I'm glad you made me do it," she admitted. Her cheeks hurt from smiling.

"I had fun, too." Michael rolled one table back into place, arranging the equipment back into order.

Ally looked out the window at the summer sun setting behind the trees. The idea of going back to her mom and Martin's place seemed terrible. She didn't want to stay with her dads. She could hit up Elizabeth, but they were all probably getting ready for bed.

She looked out at Michael. "Want to go to the tavern for a quick drink?"

He looked up from wiping the last table. "I don't drink."

"Oh, sorry." She felt suddenly stupid for asking. "I was just looking for something to do before heading home, that's all. It's weird not having my own place."

"My buddies and I have a card game tonight, if you want to join us."

"As a friend, right, not like… anything else?"

He gave her a look.

"I'm not trying to be insulting." She raised her chin. "I just haven't really talked about my boyfriend all that much."

"You mean you didn't talk about Jean-Paul's Parisian bakery all night, with every single group?"

"I didn't talk about him with *everyone*," she mumbled under her breath.

He rolled his eyes. "Well, your highness, you did a good job. You shouldn't bother talking about anybody's baking but your own."

She rolled her eyes, but she recognized the compliment. "So, where's this game?"

"Over at my buddy Harry's place."

"Harry Weisman, from high school?"

"Yeah." He looked surprised that she remembered him.

"With real money?"

"No, we use make-believe money."

She gave him a look.

"Of course, real money." He shook his head. "I can pick you up in an hour."

"Is this a formal affair?"

"Yes, Princess, you might want to wear your crown."

"I was just asking." She shook her head. "I'll go, but only if you pick me up on that fancy motorcycle of yours."

He lifted an eyebrow. "Do you think you can handle such a ride?"

"Totally."

She raced home and showered, excited about the idea of riding a motorcycle. She grabbed her best pair of jeans and stole Elise's leather jacket that she'd picked up thirty years ago at Galeries Lafayette. Just as she pulled out the hairdryer, her phone rang. It was Jean-Paul. She looked at the time. She had twenty-minutes, hardly enough time to talk and get ready. She hesitated, but then answered.

"Hey, you miss me," she teased.

"Oui." He sounded short. "I had a minute before going in this morning."

It was three in the morning, his time. "You're going in early."

"Yes, well, my sous chef is in the States."

Her stomach twisted with guilt. "Oh, I didn't realize you had to change your schedule so much."

Her cheeks warmed as she stood with her hair dripping. She had wanted to tell him about the class and how well it went. Maybe he, too, could run classes. Maybe she could run them. But she didn't. Instead she said, "Do you need me to come back?"

He didn't say anything, and the more time ticked away, the more anxious she became.

"No." He let out a sigh. "You should be with your family. I will be okay."

"I can come back sooner than my original plan. My dad's

doing really well, but he just came home from the hospital, and I'd like to make sure they're all set before I leave."

She also sighed. She wasn't even sure Frank would ask.

"I miss you, mon amour." He sounded exhausted more than anything. "Come back as soon as you can."

She didn't mention the card game and the motorcycle ride.

When she said goodbye to Jean-Paul, she had only a few minutes to spare before Michael arrived. She ran around and pulled her hair up into a wet messy bun right before she saw a single headlight in her parents' driveway.

"I'll be home later," Ally said to Elise and Martin as they watched television in the living room. She felt sixteen.

"Make sure you bring a key!" Elise said as Ally stepped outside.

Michael came up the walkway with a helmet in his hands. Ally looked out at the beautiful motorcycle sitting in the driveway. She squealed. "I've always wanted to ride an Indian FTR!"

She grabbed the helmet out of his hands and put it on as she ran toward the bike.

Michael climbed on first, not hiding his surprise. "You know what kind of bike this is?"

"Do you not expect a woman to know?"

"No, I expected *you* not to know."

She gave him a face as she put on her helmet. "What's that supposed to mean?"

He got on, ignoring her as he started the engine. She jumped on the back, wrapping her arms around his waist, feeling a bit guilty that she hadn't told Jean-Paul, but it wasn't like she was doing anything wrong. It was just a bike ride.

With a hot Marine.

Michael started the engine and pulled out of the driveway and down the road. The lights of Camden Cove twinkled over the harbor. The ride was smooth as he took the corners and drove through town, the summer heat coming up off the pavement. The wind felt warm against her skin as he cruised down Main Street and swung a left up Pleasant, hitting the hill and going straight up and out of town. She looked behind, watching the town and water disappear.

But then Michael sped up and weaved through the windy, wooded roads, the pines and maples too dark to decipher. She could barely see a thing. Each time a car came from the other direction she'd hide her head against his back and squeeze her eyes shut.

Ten minutes later, she held on for dear life as they finally made it to Harry's place, a tiny bungalow situated along the Camden River. Ally jumped off the bike as soon as Michael stopped and took off the helmet. She had never been happier to be on the ground than she was at that moment. She pulled out her bun, shaking her hair out. She didn't even care what she looked like, just happy to be alive. She handed over the helmet to Michael, who stood staring at her.

"What? Do I have a bug in my teeth?" She picked at her front tooth with a nail that felt especially dry.

He shook his head then put the helmet on the bike. "The guys are inside."

$$\sim$$

Michael couldn't keep his eyes off Ally. When she tossed her hair after getting off his bike, he had to physically stop his mouth from dropping open. At that moment, he knew he was in trouble.

As they got closer to the door, he noticed Ally's expression change.

"Do they mind I'm here?" Ally asked, looking into the window. "Maybe you should have texted him again."

"No, Harry never checks his phone, he'll be cool." A loud cheer came from inside, followed by clapping. Michael smiled. "Everyone's here."

He opened the door, praying no one would give him a hard time about Ally being with him. Sully and Harry had their backs toward the entrance, facing the television as the Red Sox played the bottom of the eighth.

"Hey guys," Michael said, motioning Ally to follow him inside.

"How was your playdate with Queen Hottie..?" Sully's voice trailed off as Ally stepped inside.

Harry laughed at Sully's blunder, but just sat and stared at her.

"Hey, Mikey, you brought company." Sully's Irish face glowed red.

"I found an extra player." Harry and Sully stared at Ally. "You all remember Ally, right?"

"Well, how could we forget Miss Homecoming?" Sully took the lead, turning on the charm. He offered a seat as Harry continued to stare.

"Thanks." Ally sat on the couch.

"All done teaching our Mikey here how to bake, then?" Sully asked, sitting next to her. No one intimidated Sully. Harry, however, still hadn't greeted her.

"Sort of, we actually have more to do." Ally crossed her legs as she talked, folding her hands over her knee. Michael couldn't tell if she was completely comfortable, or ready to run for it.

Sully cleared his throat with authority. "Is he being a difficult student?"

Harry's mouth opened, but Michael shot him a look before a smart remark came out.

"Michael's a great chef. He doesn't really need my help. It's mostly my dad's lack of organization that's the problem," Ally said, becoming comfortable with having Sully inches away.

Sully asked Ally one ridiculous question after another with Harry joining in occasionally with a nod. In no time, Ally seemed to fit right in.

"I thought you guys were going to play some cards?" she asked Sully.

"Well, Harry here forgot to make the dip, so we decided to watch the game."

Michael threw a pillow at Harry. "You forgot the dip?"

Harry threw it back. "Sorry! I had someone come to the bookstore and take up my time."

"Ally, you're more than welcome to join our next game over at my place, next week," Sully offered. "My wife makes a killer dip."

She smiled her fantastic smile. "Thanks, I'll keep that in mind, but Michael and I brought some pastries."

Michael set the box on the coffee table. "I figured you'd forget the dip."

"I didn't forget the mojitos," Harry said, standing. "I'll go get them."

"I can help." Ally followed Harry into the kitchen. "I'd love a mojito."

"I have a ton of mint in my garden." Harry told her the recipe as they disappeared into the other room.

Sully hit him in the arm. "Do you think I've aged well?"

Michael laughed. "No."

Sully hit him again, harder. "Ha, ha." He rubbed his shaved head. "I've lost the hair since high school."

Sully had once been known for his long locks.

"You look great, man."

"I can't believe you all hang out together, still." She walked back to the living room with a drink in her hand and took a seat next to Sully again. She opened the box of pastries and pushed them in front of everyone. "So, Sully, you're going to be a dad."

"Yup. A baby boy."

"That's wonderful." She sipped her drink. "My cousin Elizabeth is having a baby, too."

"Yeah, she and Adam were in our Lamaze class."

Ally looked surprised, then shook her head. "I forget how small it is here."

Harry sat in the recliner. "Michael told us you live in Paris."

"Yes, I've lived there for a couple of years." She took another sip. "This is delicious."

"There's coffee brewed in the kitchen," Harry said to Michael, who leaned over to the table to grab a pastry.

Michael nodded at his friend and headed to the kitchen. He opened the cupboard, grabbing a mug. As he poured his coffee, he thought that if this had been high school, no one would ever believe that the homecoming queen, the biggest nerd, and the anonymous derelicts were all hanging out. How things changed.

"So, do you play poker?" Harry asked, seemingly interested, as Michael looked on from the kitchen.

She shrugged. "No, but it's better than watching Masterpiece Theatre with my parents."

Michael liked the idea of a family hanging out, watching something together. He always assumed families were like his, dysfunctional. He had no memories of his parents ever getting along. Plus, his dad was gone for most of his childhood.

"They watch those period dramas things." Ally shivered.

Sully leaned back on the couch, closer to Ally. "Hanging out with us is definitely a better option."

"Watch out for Michael then, he's a card shark," Harry warned her.

"I heard that," Michael said, returning with his cup of coffee.

He noticed Ally watching him as he came in from the kitchen. Her blonde hair was tossed over to one side, her tank top showing off her shoulders, a dangerous beauty.

What was happening right now?

CHAPTER 7

*a*lly should probably have said no to the second mojito. But she had been having such a good time, and she couldn't refuse Harry, especially since he needed to finish off the pitcher. Michael drove her on the motorcycle through the woods and she felt like she was flying like an owl across the sky, the stars streaking against the black velvet night above them.

Her head pounded the next day, but when she saw Michael, she pretended to feel great the second he gave her a hard time.

"How's that second mojito now?"

"Ha, ha," she said, but secretly checked her breath in the pantry, making sure she didn't smell like alcohol. He didn't let on that she had acted like an idiot, in fact, he said she fit right in with his friends.

"It's not every day we have royalty among us." He was teasing, she knew, but she hoped he'd enjoyed himself as well.

Frank came bursting in, frantic.

"I need help on the counter." He typed on his phone as he spoke. "Brittany called in sick."

"I can," she volunteered.

Frank continued to type. "I could probably call Kate."

"I'm fine in the kitchen," Michael said.

Ally could feel her face warm in anger at Frank's blatant disregard of her offer. Did he really not want her around?

Then he dropped his arms to his side. "That would be wonderful, Ally. Thank you."

I broke him, she thought to herself. On the other side of the kitchen, she saw Michael smile.

The rest of the day had been busy, being a weekend. Customers poured in from the hot summer sun for iced coffee and a pastry. Frank talked to them all. Even the customers she was ringing up. Everyone seemed completely at ease with him, but there she stood, only feet away from her stepfather, and none of his friendly banter was directed at her. Frank actually seemed uncomfortable when he spoke to her, as though he didn't know what to say.

When Harry stopped in, she was glad to see him. She had really enjoyed herself last night, and it made being in Camden Cove more tolerable. Throughout the night, she and Harry had talked about art and music, about traveling and school, and also about places to go when she was in town. He even offered to go with her to Boston. No one brought up the Ally of yesteryear, well, except a jab from Michael here and there, but if anything, it broke the ice with Harry and Sully. Ally wanted them to understand that the old Ally was gone forever.

Harry passed a book to her before grabbing a cup of coffee. "Can you give this to Michael?"

"Does he ever read anything that's not dismal?" She fanned through the thick book of *War and Peace* with her thumb.

"He's going through a classics stage. One time he had this memoir phase and—" Harry stopped talking as a woman walked in through the door. "Eve."

"Harry!" The woman had midnight black hair above her shoulders, with sharply cut bangs. She wore dark rimmed glasses just like he did, and smiled sweetly when she saw him.

"It's nice to see you." Harry's cheeks flashed bright pink.

"Good to see you, too."

Ally saw what was happening. Harry had a crush.

"I was just about to go to the bookstore," Eve said.

"Oh, I'm sorry I'm going to miss you." Harry stood there, not noticing what Ally did, that Eve also had a thing for Harry. "Tom will help you find what you're looking for."

Eve nodded and said, "Maybe I'll see you soon."

"Yes, I'd like that." Harry waved as Eve walked to the end of the line.

As soon as she was out of earshot, Ally leaned over the counter and said to him, "Harry, take these cups and pastries," she whispered, "and ask her to sit with you."

"I couldn't do that." Harry tried to hand back the extra cup, but Ally pushed it at him.

"Yes, you can."

Frank grabbed a few pastry puffs and said, "Ask her if you can walk her back to the bookstore."

Ally was surprised he had been paying enough attention to understand what was going on.

"What?" Frank shrugged. "I love a little romance."

Harry's eyes shot open and it all finally clicked. "Oh!" Harry looked back at Eve, then asked warily "Do you really think she'll want to have coffee with me?"

"Yes." Ally pushed him away with a tap on his shoulder. "Now, get over there."

Harry slowly approached Eve, who smiled as soon as he held up the extra cup. Ally and Frank watched as the two headed to the coffee station and started talking.

She turned to say something to Frank, but he was already helping the next customer.

After the rush dwindled down, she headed to the kitchen with another empty tray and dumped it in the sink. Her head felt heavy.

"Ally, you saved the day!" Frank said, as he walked into the kitchen.

Michael stood in front of the island with a tray of macarons.

He seemed to be ahead of demand. He hardly needed her help at this point.

"I'm glad I could help."

"Well, I think we're okay for now. Why don't you take off and relax?"

"I don't mind helping—"

"No, Ally, go. Enjoy the rest of the day."

Ally looked at Michael and saw understanding in his eyes. "Um, okay." She wiped her hands on a dish towel. "I'll just leave, then."

"Yes, please, go do something fun. Maybe stop by to see your Dad. He'd love to see you."

"Is he upset that I haven't come today?" she asked, wondering if she wasn't spending enough time with him.

"No, but I'm sure you'd much rather do that than work in our little kitchen."

Frank picked up a tray of croissants. "I'll bring these out, you go."

"Okay."

Frank swung through to the front, saying goodbye as he went.

"So, I guess I'll get going." She picked up her purse and gave Michael a wave.

"Ally, you know he's trying to be nice, right?"

"I should go." She stalked out, but stopped at the radio and pointed. "Ugh, turn off that country."

Michael could tell the interaction between Frank and Ally had been awkward for both of them. It was for him, too. Frank never seemed to be short on words, except when it came to Ally. Or maybe he'd noticed something strange between the two of them because she'd pointed it out to him. Nevertheless, it had been weird.

After the lunch rush, Frank insisted Michael go home early,

too. "You've been working like crazy. I hope Ally was able to help you out."

"Yeah, she's really good." Michael took off his apron, dropping it inside his bag.

"She really is, isn't she?" Frank walked around the kitchen, cleaning up, rearranging things. He squeezed the dishtowel he held. "How was the class?"

"It went great."

Frank nodded. He looked at Michael. "You get her."

"Excuse me?"

"Not many people get Ally, but you seem to."

"What do you mean?"

"Her father and I begged her to work here for years, yet you ask, and now we can't get her out of here."

"I think she thought you'd ask, actually."

"She wants us to ask?" Frank looked puzzled. He took a seat on the stool by the counter. "I thought she didn't want anything to do with the place."

Michael had a feeling this whole thing was one big miscommunication. How many times had he and his mother gotten into a fight over something as stupid as this? How he wished he could fight with his mother again. "Look, it's none of my business."

Frank looked up.

"Never mind." Michael zipped up his bag and threw it on his shoulder.

"No, what?" Frank asked, sitting up on the stool.

"I think she feels out of place, since you keep telling her you don't need her help."

"But we didn't want to burden her." Frank's forehead scrunched.

"But she came all this way *to* help."

Frank face grew thoughtful. "So, she *wants* to help?"

"Yeah."

Frank let Michael's information simmer, then said, "Well, thanks, Michael."

"Sure thing." Michael saluted him, shutting the door behind him as he left.

He headed up the street to Harry's bookstore. He'd grab a new book for his mom, then maybe some groceries. When he opened the door and stepped inside, he heard a familiar voice. He made his way through the small cramped shop to the back office and there, sitting with Harry, was Ally.

"What are you doing here?" he asked.

"I thought I'd come and get my dad a new book." She held up a clutch of novels. "I found a lot of great titles."

Michael smiled. Of course, Harry would hook her up.

"What are you looking for now?" Harry asked Michael.

"I came to find something for my mom."

"I have a few new large print on the back wall," he said. Then he turned his attention to Ally. "Do you think it would be cheesy if I asked her to go letterboxing?"

"Absolutely not, no." Ally squeezed her hands together over her chest. "She would love it, if that's what she enjoys doing."

Michael stopped midway down the book aisle. What were they talking about?

"Oh, I don't know," Harry said. "She might just like books."

"No one likes books that much," Ally said. "If she comes in all the time... and there was no mistaking the look she was giving you in the bakery."

What were they talking about? Or *who*, would be the better question.

"What are you two up to?" he asked.

"It's nothing." Harry shook his head. "It's silly, really, I think I'm just getting the signals wrong or something." He waved his hand in the air.

"No, Harry, you're not. Ask her." Ally's eyes narrowed at Michael, scrutinizing him. "Don't pay attention to him."

"What's that supposed to mean?" Michael said, offended, but not exactly sure why, since no one was telling him anything.

"Well, the minute you walked back here, Harry started

changing his mind and chickening out."

"I'm not chickening out," Harry said.

"Chickening out about what?"

"Chickening out on asking Eve out."

"I haven't chickened out—"

Michael interrupted. "Who's Eve?"

"She's just a customer."

"See!" Ally shook her head. "Maybe if you looked for a book, instead of eavesdropping, then Harry wouldn't chicken out."

"How is it my fault that Harry's chicken?"

"I haven't chickened out!" Harry brushed his shirt sleeve and said, "Eve is a woman who comes into the shop."

Michael and Harry's friendship had started in grammar school. In all those years, he didn't remember Harry ever asking a woman out. He'd been on dates where the woman asked, or the occasional setup here and there. But Harry had always been too shy and quiet.

"Ask her to go letterboxing, and then take her to lunch," Ally suggested.

"I don't know."

"Take her to Ally's class," Michael said.

Harry cocked his head. "Ally's class?"

"Oh, that's perfect!" Ally jumped in her seat. "You could bring a bottle of wine."

"And then grab coffee afterwards, and sit by the harbor at the tables," he added.

"I don't know. What would we talk about?"

"We'll be there," Ally said.

Michael looked at her. "We?"

"Yes, I need your help." Ally gave him a look, a look that made his stomach do a belly flop.

Dang, she did something to him. He shook his head.

"Okay, that sounds perfect." Harry smiled. "I think I'll ask her, then."

"In the class tomorrow, we're baking macarons." Ally clapped her hands together. "It'll be a perfect first date."

Michael nodded, but once again felt unbalanced around Ally Williams. Something about that woman would be no good for his very stable, very routine life, especially since she had someone named Jean-Paul waiting for her in Paris.

~

As Harry dialed Eve's number, Ally walked the aisles, looking at the titles. She couldn't remember the last time she sat down and read a book. What was the last book she'd read? She tilted her head to the side to get a better look at the spines. She pulled out a few more titles to add to her pile, then walked to the counter.

Harry's bookshop did not hold true to its name, it was not 'mainly mysteries'. Every type of book filled the tiny space. There were a lot of great titles, old and new.

Michael stood at the counter with his own stack of books. She dumped her pile next to his.

"What are you reading?" he asked.

She looked at the pile. "These are just for my dad."

"You're not getting anything for yourself?"

She shook her head. "I can't find anything."

"You can't find anything?" Michael huffed as he gestured to the overfilled bookshelves. "What do you like to read?"

"Magazines?" She knew this was not the right answer for him. "Cookbooks."

"Go back and find a book for you." Michael pointed to the shelves behind her, shaking his head, mumbling, "*Magazines*."

"At least they're not depressing, and make me want to jump off a cliff."

"If literary classics make you feel that way, then by all means stick with *People*."

She huffed. "I like more uplifting pieces for my leisure reading." She looked at his stack. "I mean *1984*, really?"

"I'm sure reading gossip about people you don't know is really

77

uplifting." He shook his head. "Silly me, wanting to expand my mind."

"If that's what you call it." She was pretty sure he liked to expand his ego. "I just don't have time to read."

He threw a book at her. "Tell me you don't start weeping like a baby. Plus, there's a movie to go with it."

"The *Art of Racing in the Rain?*"

Ally looked at the cover, turning it around to read the back.

"You coming in, tomorrow?"

She shrugged, then shook her head. "Frank won't need me."

"I do."

She looked up at him. "No, you don't."

He passed another book over to her, *My Life in France* by Julia Child. "Yes, I do."

Michael grabbed his pile and left. Ally's mouth gaped as she tried to formulate words, but she couldn't come up with any. Why did her whole body feel like it was floating?

As she left the bookshop, she started to read the first page of the book with the dog on the cover. By the time she reached the beach, she had finished the first chapter. She took a seat on the bench by the harbor, kicking off her flip-flops, and read for the first time in years.

After a couple of hours, and on account of her butt being sore and numb, she left the bench and went to the diner to grab a bite to eat. She sat at the counter and read. She didn't put the book down until she went to bed at her mom's. Then she woke up only to pick up the book before she got ready. Enzo suddenly felt more real to her than some of the people in her life.

She opened the bakery, turning on the ovens with the book in her hand.

"I told you," Michael said as he walked in, the sky still dark.

She turned to face him with tears in her eyes. "Are you kidding me?"

She threw the book down on the kitchen counter.

He laughed at her dramatics. "What?"

"I know what's about to come, but I don't want to read it!"

He nodded, as though he knew exactly what she meant.

"I should've known when I saw the dog on the cover."

"I needed to prove my point."

"How does making me cry expand my mind?"

"It makes you reflect on yourself as a person." He shrugged. "You can't get through a book without relating to it somehow."

The corner of his mouth perked up at her before he turned back to the refrigerator, pulling out the pastries that had been prepped the night before.

The morning went smoothly. Michael didn't need any help. He could easily take over the baking at this point, but she enjoyed coming, so she was glad he kept asking her. Kate came in the early morning, looking exhausted.

"I stayed up all night with a new client, working on a website design." She rubbed her eyes.

"I can take the counter if you want to go home and rest."

"Really?" Kate looked thrilled. "That would be so great, Ally."

It wasn't until Frank showed up that she regretted telling Kate to go home. He immediately stiffened up. Maybe she was imagining things, like her mom would say.

"How's Dad?" she asked.

"He's tired, but okay." Frank looked exhausted. "The visiting nurse is coming this afternoon."

"Do you need help?"

Frank started to shake his head, and her heart dropped. Of course not.

"You know, I'd love some help."

Ally looked up. "Really?"

"Yes, I'd love it if you could help close up," Frank said. "But I understand if you can't, since you've been here all day."

"I can," she said eagerly.

"And tomorrow I might need some help with your dad, too."

She looked into the kitchen, and Michael looked up at her. He smiled. She couldn't help but smile back.

CHAPTER 8

*A*lly got to the bakery earlier than she told Michael to meet her, but he was already there. She found it funny that he was so competitive. She was almost certain he was *trying* to get there before her. She swung the door open and the ingredients were already out on the counter.

"Today, cakes," she said, as she tied her apron around her waist. She was going to teach Michael how David baked his signature cakes, or really her grandmother Grace's signature cakes. She pulled her hair back with a silk headscarf. Her favorite, one of her Grandma Grace's scarves, or GG as the grandkids called her. GG had given it to Ally one day before church. She'd wrapped it around her head and tied a bow just below her ear.

"You look beautiful," GG had said, turning Ally toward the mirror.

That, coming from her grandmother, who she thought looked like Jaqueline Kennedy, meant that maybe someday she'd grow up to be just as beautiful.

"It's all about the timing," Ally said to Michael.

Once they started, Michael didn't wait long before he added

his own spin to some of the ingredients for the cakes. "I'd like to put a little higher ratio of butter in the batter."

Ally trusted his changes, curious to taste the results.

As they worked, they moved in sync with one another, the precision almost comedic. Ally smiled to herself, wondering if he felt it, too, that they were a good team.

"You want to stock the front while I load the van?" Michael asked. He had already boxed most of the pastries for Elizabeth's baby shower. Ally grabbed a cookie sheet filled with fresh eclairs and slid the tray into the refrigerated glass case. She flipped on the lights. A ray of sun peeked through the front window, making the room glow a soft peachy orange.

Ally looked back and watched Michael. She wondered why he wasted his talent being an assistant chef to her cousin Jack. He had a real gift in the kitchen, more talent than most. He could run his own kitchen. He certainly had the drive. Didn't the military give G.I. Joe something or other for education? He could easily get training in Portland or Boston for that matter.

What was holding him back?

The rest of the morning flew by, and before she knew it, Michael drove her over to her Aunt Sarah's house for the shower in the delivery van. Her cousin Lauren greeted them outside and grabbed some boxes, carrying them into the house and setting them on the counter. Pink and blue balloons, an inflatable stork, and a handcrafted cradle filled with diapers sat in the middle of room. Ally's stomach soured.

Sarah fluttered over to them from the other side of the room.

"Thank you so much!" Sarah kissed Ally on the cheek and grabbed the cake box out of her hands. She pointed to the table overflowing with finger foods. "Michael, go grab yourself a plate of food and take it with you."

Michael held up his hand. "I'm all set, but thanks."

"It works out perfectly you're here!"

Sarah fluttered away again and before Ally could stop herself, she said, "You're coming back afterwards to pick up the platters and stuff, right?"

He gave her a look and shrugged. "Sure. When would you like me to come back?"

She looked at the clock. "No more than three hours."

If the shower had been just the Williams women, Frank, and the usual suspects, then she wouldn't rush out. But her aunt's living room was filled with extended family and locals from town. People who'd keep asking "when was it her turn" to get married and start a family. So many "expected" her to be married already, and were "shocked" to hear she was still single.

"No ring?" Lauren teased, stepping up to her with a glass of white wine.

"You are a godsend." She sipped the cool drink, then joked, "How are you still single?"

"Ha, ha." Lauren pointed her glass at Sarah, who was talking to Frank and Elizabeth. "It's really the look of pity on the married-with-children women, as though life isn't complete without the ring and the baby Bjorn."

Ally spit out some of her wine when a voice called out from the door.

"I'm here!" Christine Winters squealed as she walked into the family room.

"Oh, Lord, Christine showed up," Lauren muttered as she walked away.

"It's five in Paris," Ally mumbled to herself as she took another sip. She watched as Christine rearranged Sarah's diaper cake centerpiece.

"What did you say?" Michael had snuck up behind her.

Ally jumped so high she almost lost her drink, but Michael held out his hand and steadied her. "Oh my god! You almost gave me a heart attack. Don't sneak up on people like that."

"Why, 'cause they'll hear what you're mumbling to yourself?"

"Yes. Exactly."

Michael laughed. "So, I'll be back."

Ally held up her drink.

He shot her a thumb's up, and left.

"Was Michael always really hot?" Lauren said from behind her.

Ally jumped again, looking away from Michael's backside. "Has everyone decided to just sneak up instead of letting someone you know you're coming? But yes, he's always been that hot."

"I think he likes you," she said.

"No, he's just a really nice guy who's helping my dads."

"Yes, but also really hot."

"Don't you have a boyfriend?" Ally wanted this conversation over.

"Do you think you and Jean-Paul are ever going to get–"

"Lauren!" Ally cut her off. She couldn't believe she was turning out like all the others. "Don't you go and start."

"Sorry, wow, you're right." Lauren shook her head. "I really sounded like my mom right there."

They both looked at Sarah, who was shushing everyone. "Elizabeth's coming up the driveway. Hide, everyone!"

Ally looked at the crowd of at least forty people in the open room. The women hid behind the couch or the counters in the kitchen, or stepped into the hallways.

Lucy and Adam walked her in and everyone jumped out of their hiding spots.

"Surprise!"

Elizabeth covered her face with both hands and immediately started to cry, burying her face in Adam's chest. Lucy jumped up and down, clapping her hands as Sarah ushered her into the room. The crowd started laughing and clapping as Elizabeth recognized the faces.

"I can't believe you all pulled this off!" she said, laughing and wiping away her tears.

Ally kept a smile frozen on her face, but inside she wanted to crawl away and avoid the next three hours of reminiscing about horrifying births as though they were happy memories.

Food and drinks were served first, followed by a few games, where Ally won first prize by putting a diaper on a bag of flour the fastest.

When she finished her wine, she started talking to Frank about Michael. "I just don't understand why he's not trying to go into Boston or somewhere to work at a restaurant."

"Well, I'm sure he's staying here to take care of his mom."

"His mom?" A vision of his tattoo floated in her head.

"She's living over in Majestic Oaks."

Ally had been a volunteer at the nursing home as a teenager. "Isn't she young to be living there?"

"She was diagnosed with early onset Alzheimer's when he was out on deployment." Frank, of course, knew the whole story. She was surprised that Michael had never mentioned it, while all she did was complain about her own problems with Frank.

"I didn't know."

"He's all she has at this point."

"The cake is so good!" Adam's mother said, as she took her second slice. "Perfect for a wedding."

"Oh, good," Ally said, grabbing the gift notebook from Lauren's hands for something to do. "What'd you get, Elizabeth?"

"It's a baby wipes warmer!" Elizabeth squealed along with all the others.

"I can't believe you and Adam don't want to find out," Lauren complained. "I'd want to decorate in colors other than green or yellow."

"We're going to wait until the baby comes." Elizabeth rubbed her belly and Ally had to force herself not to roll her eyes, suddenly irritated by the cuteness of the whole affair. Soft yellows and greens filled the room with tiny little jumpers and itty-bitty hats. The socks were even more adorable. Everything had a theme of some sort of farm animal.

Ally couldn't wait for it to be over.

"Oh, Christine, the blanket is beautiful!" Elizabeth held up a knitted blanket for the whole crowd of friends and neighbors to see.

"It took me forty-two hours. Almost as long as I was in labor!" Christine bragged as she looked over to Ally. She'd been doing that since she got to the shower.

"Wow," Ally said under her breath as she wrote down the gift next to Christine's name. "Bet she'll talk about it for forty-two more."

Once Elizabeth finished opening the presents and people started to leave, Ally walked around, grabbing glasses and plates, picking up any random silverware. Some of her aunts and cousins were still sitting around talking about the joys of being married and having children. First, it was GG who told the tale of the boys being born, then her Aunt Sarah told the horror story of when Matt got "stuck and blue". Then Elise told her story of how perfect the delivery had been in Paris with Ally. As the story went, Ally had been rip roaring and ready to go.

She never had been more thankful than she was when Michael came walking in from the back with Matthew, because she was rip roaring and ready to go.

"Michael!" She instantly perked up, rushing to him with a tray full of plates. "Let me go with you to bring this stuff back."

She didn't even wait for his response, just rushed out of the happiest place on earth. She stuffed the trays in the back of the van and jumped into the passenger's seat, avoiding having to go back inside.

"Not going to say goodbye?" he asked, as he put the rest of the items in the back.

She shook her head as he made a face.

"Don't you think that's rude?"

She gave him a look. "Let me feel sorry for myself for a little bit, alright?"

He got into the van and reversed it down the driveway. "Sure you don't want to say goodbye?"

"Believe me, they won't even notice I'm gone." Ally may have sounded like she felt sorry for herself, but she was almost certain they wouldn't. "Besides, I want to get ready for the cooking class tonight."

"Elizabeth might think you're upset with her."

"I'll text an apology later." Ally folded her hands together. "Please don't make me go back in there."

Michael nodded. "Still want my help for class?"

"Yes, are you kidding me?" Ally was certain his help was the only reason things went as smoothly as they did the first time.

"Gladys does like my tattoo." He rubbed his forearm of roses. "Almost as much as you did."

Ally's eyes shot open, but she didn't look at him, instead kept her gaze on the road up ahead. This was the first time he had mentioned their encounter at the wedding. The first acknowledgment of any kind. Her cheeks warmed at the thought of her rubbing his arm like Gladys.

"Oh, those Golden Girls are feisty, you better watch out for yourself," Ally said, pretending not to be suddenly hot and bothered, thinking about what Lauren said. "Mr. Martland did enjoy talking to you while rolling out his dough."

Michael let out an abrupt laugh that made Ally jump, but she smiled to herself for getting him. "Well, Princess, let's get you ready for class."

Michael couldn't help but watch Ally as she did her thing up front, walking the group through the recipe. Did she notice it? He might be freaking her out for all he knew, but there he was, eyes stuck on her like a puppy dog as she stood teaching the class. She had the attention of everyone else, too. She could work an older crowd, but also had the younger couples on their honeymoon, or first dates like Harry and Eve. She had been funny in a way everyone enjoyed, but also welcoming questions and breaks when they needed it. The group of twelve enjoyed the time together because of her.

"What's your next class going to be?" Mr. Fitzpatrick asked from his wife's side. He had been there mostly as the sampler.

"I won't be teaching that one, I'll be headed back by then."

Michael's stomach lurched, sweeping up his breath. "You're going back in a week?"

"In five days, actually." She looked at her phone. "So, now you're going to fold your almond mixture into those stiff glossy peaks, about thirty strokes. But be gentle and extra careful."

As the groups folded the mixture into the batter, Ally walked around. She appeared completely at ease with the group, talking to each table, enjoying the conversation. Did she have something better than this in Paris? Michael wanted to ask her. Then he remembered... his name was Jean-Paul.

Harry sat motionless at the table with Eve, who was the only one folding. He saw her try to ask a question, but Harry didn't give much in return. He decided it might be best to check on things and help his buddy out.

"How's your batter?" Michael looked into the silver mixing bowl. Eve had created a perfect macaron batter. "That looks great."

Harry nodded with him, but said nothing.

"Hey, Harry, why don't you come with me to get some more vanilla." Michael grabbed his friend under his arm before he had a chance to answer and pulled him to the pantry.

"What are you doing?" Harry hissed as Michael closed the door.

"What are *you* doing?" Michael asked. "I thought you liked this girl?"

"I do." Harry flung up his hands as though it was obvious.

"Then why do you look so depressed?"

"I don't—"

"You do." He wouldn't let him argue. "You haven't spoken a word since you got here."

"I don't know what to say."

"You ask questions about her, what she thinks about stuff, get to know her by asking about her job, her childhood. You could even talk about books."

"If you know so much, then why are you not dating anyone?"

"Because I don't want to deal with this kind of stuff." Michael grabbed Harry's shoulder and spun him around toward the door. "What's something nice you could tell her?"

"She smells good."

"That's nice." Michael patted Harry on the back. "Or you could tell her something about the way she looks, like her eyes."

"She does have pretty eyes."

"Just get to know her."

"Says the guy who has women literally hanging off his arm."

"But no one under seventy." Gladys waved at him when he opened the door.

"Do you think she likes me?"

"I don't know. I'm not in fifth grade."

Harry narrowed his eyes at his friend.

"Just be yourself." Michael stuffed the jar of vanilla paste into Harry's hand and pushed him out of the pantry.

"Hey, Eve," he heard Harry say. He looked for Ally.

She stood off at the other end of the kitchen with a pair of women, but she was looking for him, too. When their eyes caught, they held on, neither backing away. She smiled, which made him smile, too. The silent conversation made his collar heat up.

Was he misreading the signals?

Was Ally Williams warming up to him?

As the class finished up, people started saying their goodbyes. All of the macarons had been baked and boxed up with a bow. Ally shook hands with each of her students and gave Harry and Eve a hug.

"Don't forget about the concert in the park."

"That sounds like fun," Eve said.

"We should all go together." Ally looked at Michael. "You in?"

He only paused for a second, and even though he saw all the red flags, he said, "Absolutely."

He was certain there was no way this would ever end well.

Michael started sweeping as Ally put all the dirty dishes into the sink to soak. She grabbed a towel, wetting it with soap, and washed off the tabletops. He walked over to David's radio and tuned it to a classic country station. Willie Nelson played in the background as he went back to sweeping.

"That went great, right?" she said, her face glowing.

"You're really good with the group," he said, resting on the handle of the broom.

She smiled. "Thanks."

She wiped another table, pushing it against the wall. "I always hated being in front of people at La Patisserie Michalak. I would stand behind this glass, with people staring at me. I forget they're there half the time, and I'm just in my head thinking of the next task, and go to itch my nose and people are staring at me."

"Sounds very different."

"I feel like I'm in a zoo."

"Hmmm." He swept again, making a pile in the middle of the floor. "You should open your own place, or you could always work here."

"My Dad doesn't need me now." She jumped up on the counter, leaning back on her arms. "I wouldn't mind teaching. I really like that."

"You should start your own English version of French cooking classes, you know, for expats and stuff." Michael leaned down and swept the broom under the stove. "I bet you'd find a ton of people to take your classes."

"Maybe…" She looked out past him. He could tell she was contemplating it. "That would be cool to do, if I could find people who'd want to do it."

"You should create a cookbook for your classes. You have all the recipes written out." Michael pointed the handle of the broom at David's computer. You could be the next Julia Childs."

"Or David Lebovitz!"

"Yeah, that guy."

Her eyes grew large with dreams. She walked across the kitchen with vigor in her step and grabbed the laptop off the counter. "I could talk to my dad about the recipes we've gone through. Plus, I have my own recipes at home."

"You have more?"

"*So* much more."

Michael clapped his hands together and pointed at her. "That's exactly what you should do!"

She bit her thumb as a smile played across her face. "I'm totally going to start planning out my book tonight!"

She jumped up off the counter and ran to him, giving him a big hug, squeezing her arms around his waist. She leaned back, her face so close to his that he could smell rose oil from the nape of her neck. He lifted his chin to meet hers and moved in to kiss her. She kissed him quickly on the cheek, then scooted away out of the kitchen. "I'll see you tomorrow!"

He dropped the broom and took a seat, gathering himself. Not only had he misread the whole situation, but she'd left him with all the dirty dishes.

Ally called Jean-Paul to tell him about all her new ideas. It was early morning there, maybe five o'clock, but he'd be awake by now, if not already at the bakery. The phone, however, went straight to voicemail.

"Jean-Paul, it's me again," she sounded desperate. "I had this marvelous idea for a cooking class. I'd love to run it by you. Maybe even a cookbook."

She hung up, looking out the window. Sleep eluded her again. Ally wasn't a person who needed a lot of sleep. Her energy usually ran high during the last hours of the night or the early morning. She fed off the moon.

In an old journal she found in her childhood desk, she wrote down her ideas, starting with her favorite recipe, David's croissant. The simple, yet complex, buttery pastry had always been her favorite. Then she moved to macarons, thinking of the night with Michael. She hadn't felt that good in a kitchen in a *long* time. She took a chance he'd be awake, too, and texted him.

Her phone lit up. **Be there in five.**

Ally slipped out of bed and got dressed. Tiptoeing downstairs as quietly as she could, she tried to remember which of the stairs creaked, so she wouldn't wake her mom and Martin. It was the cat's fault she screamed in the kitchen. To be fair, Leo gave no warning at all before attacking her ankles.

The headlights streamed across the living room and she opened the front door, running down the sidewalk in her clogs. It felt like she was sneaking out of the house, like back in the old days with Elizabeth. Except now, it was with a guy on a motorcycle, and not a ten speed. He handed her a helmet as she climbed on behind him.

"I'm surprised you were up," she razzed him, knowing full well he'd already be at the bakery if he wasn't picking her up.

"I'm surprised you're done feeling sorry for yourself."

"Not yet," she said over the engine, as he drove faster toward town. She hugged his stomach, a very intimate gesture once she thought about it. Now feeling a bit uneasy about how she was keeping Jean-Paul out of the loop.

He slowed the bike down as he pulled in behind the bakery. The engine cut to the waves lapping against the shore off in the distance, and a boat's bell rattling in the harbor. He pulled his helmet off, pushing the kickstand down.

She climbed off and removed her own helmet, her hair lopsided on her head. She reached in and pulled out the soft pink rose-print scarf she'd bought in Paris.

"Roses, this time?" he asked.

"What? You don't like roses?" she teased.

"No, I sort of have a thing for them." He stared into her eyes with a heat that warmed her whole body.

Her heart skipped a beat.

Her phone started vibrating. She glanced down. It was Jean-Paul.

Holy moly.

She looked back at Michael, but he had already left to go inside. Was that something? Or was she misreading the situation.

She switched on the lights as she headed to the fridge, leaving the door open a bit longer to cool off. She pulled out a few containers of the ripest, darkest raspberries she'd seen all summer. "Today, I think we should bake mille-feuilles."

Michael pulled out the necessary cookware. "Sounds great."

CHAPTER 9

The smell of Harry's aftershave overpowered Michael's mother's living room as he watched Harry check himself again in the mirror. He ran a fine comb through his hair, slicking it back with what seemed like a whole tube of gel.

"I'm going with the Gordon Hayward look." Harry seemed unsure that he'd pulled it off.

"Are you going to be done before the night is over?" Michael asked.

"I think I made a mistake with this gel."

Michael rolled his eyes, but didn't mention how he'd taken three tries to find something halfway decent to wear. He'd never worried about such things before, and was annoyed at himself for caring. There wasn't the slightest chance that a piece of clothing would make a difference with a woman like Ally.

Harry snapped his fingers and pointed at the mirror. "Let's roll."

Michael shook his head as he followed Harry out of the house and into his truck. He had offered to drive everyone, and would pick up Ally next.

"I've always wanted to see what this place looked like." Harry leaned forward over the dash when they pulled up the long driveway.

"I remember when it was built."

"Yeah, it's quite a house." He drove all the way to the end, waiting for the house to come into sight.

"Now, that's an ocean view."

The house clung to the cliffs overlooking the Atlantic Ocean. It had the character of an older house with its dormers and shingled siding, but the house clearly had been built recently, with all the modern amenities. It looked more like a small inn than a residence. He couldn't imagine what it was like growing up in a house like that.

Ally ran out the front door with a bag on her shoulder. She opened the front passenger door, even though Harry was sitting next to Michael.

"You need to sit in the back with Eve."

"Oh, right!" Harry jumped out and got in the back.

When Ally sat down next to Michael, he immediately smelled the familiar mosaic of scents, too many to name, but he swore he could smell Jasmine. He breathed it in before pulling into reverse.

"We'll pick up Eve, then head downtown." Ally had turned in her seat to face Harry. "Who's the band?"

"The Jack Willow Band," Michael said. Some of those guys had been friends of his dad's. All veterans, just like him. They knew what he went through, why he kept to himself. Why a night like tonight could sometimes trigger feelings of rage. Crowds, drunks… stupid people, basically. Even Camden Cove had a few, especially during tourist season.

"What kind of music?"

"Old country, folk music, maybe some blues."

"I'm going to love it." She clapped her hands.

Michael couldn't hold back his smile as Ally returned to Harry, planning out the night. "I have two blankets, and Michael will sit with me. Eve will sit with you. You should offer her a seat before sitting down. And…"

94

"What is this, 1955?" Michael asked. "He should offer her a seat?"

"Wooing is bad?" Ally looked at him as he drove. He could barely keep his eyes on the road when her eyebrow lifted up that way, with those green eyes electrifying every part of his body.

"Anyone who wants to be wooed needs to read Madame Bovary. Woo yourself."

Ally opened her mouth, then shut it. Turning to face Harry again, she jabbed her thumb toward Michael. "Who brought Flaubert, here?"

Michael let out a roar. He was going to enjoy himself tonight.

Ally laid out the blankets and did everything as planned, except she asked Eve to sit on the other blanket and pulled Michael to the ground next to her by his shirt. Eve appeared relaxed, and Ally asked her questions. One of her infamous qualities, Ally could talk to anyone, well, except for Frank. The irony of the two chatterboxes being unable to talk to one another wasn't lost on her.

Almost all of Camden Cove sat in the square as the band set up. Boats lined the harbor with people sitting on their decks, waiting for the show. The night's temperature was perfect, with a slight breeze to keep the bugs away. She recognized a lot of the faces, but some of the names were missing.

"Did you grow up in Camden Cove?" she asked Eve.

"I was born in Boston, but moved here with my mom when I was in high school."

Ally hadn't recognized her, not that it meant anything. She *had* been gone for a while now. She left right after graduation and never looked back. First to San Francisco, and then to so many different places she was sure she'd forgotten some of them. Then back to the East to proper schooling in Montreal.

Her baking life started in Quebec. She had loved living in

Montreal. It was where she came into her talent. Where Jean-Paul discovered her, and offered her a job in Paris.

The thought of Jean-Paul flashed through her head. She hadn't talked to him in a while. She hadn't been able to get hold of him all day. She didn't know if he was that busy, or if he was upset.

She looked at Michael, who was carrying on a conversation with Eve and Harry, and felt the strange, yet familiar flutter in her stomach. Would she tell Jean-Paul about it tonight? Or should she tell him how she somehow couldn't keep her eyes off Michael?

Eve turned to Ally and asked, "Where do you live in Paris?"

"Umm." Suddenly, Ally couldn't really answer. Right now, she lived in a friend's apartment, with its parquet floors and floor to ceiling windows, but she just rented a room. She couldn't afford anything else in the 18th arrondissement.

"I live in the Montmartre neighborhood, near the Basilica."

"Wow!" Eve's eyes shot open.

Ally nodded, "Yup."

"Do you love it?"

"Most of the time."

She noticed Michael listening.

"I mean, it's beautiful, no doubt," she began. "And the people are very lovely once they know you're there to experience Paris, not just pass through. My favorite thing about the city is the people."

"I've always wanted to go." She looked dreamy. "The City of Light."

"Me, too," Harry joined in. "There's the Bibliotheque Sainte-Genevieve, where Galileo, Copernicus, and Shakespeare spoke. It's in this sixth-century building. I've always wanted to see it."

"Well, you guys have a place to stay if you want."

"No way!" Eve's eyes opened further. She hit Harry on the arm, knocking him back a bit, but with a smile. "I will totally take you up on that."

Ally hoped they did. And together would be even better, since she had a strong feeling the two of them were just perfect for each other.

Ally had offered this exact invitation to dozens of people, and no one had taken her up on it. She'd love to have visitors, show them around the city, see it for the first time again. That's what she needed. To go back and see it fresh. She turned to Michael. "You should come, too."

He smiled, but didn't say anything as Harry and Eve began talking about a make-believe trip to Paris. It occurred to her that she wasn't the only world traveler among them.

"Where were you stationed?"

Michael started picking the grass on the edge of the blanket, facing the stage. "First in San Diego, then overseas."

She thought of how spoiled she had been, living off her family, traveling, while Michael had no choice about where he ended up, and faced situations even her worst nightmares couldn't compare to.

"Did you always cook?" She was embarrassed by her behavior when she first came home. Thinking that cooking in the military wasn't as dignified as her Masters in Culinary Arts.

He shook his head. "No, I didn't start cooking until after I got injured."

"Oh." He had been injured?

"I didn't want to go out on disability and I wasn't ready to leave, so I became a cook."

So many questions burned on the tip of her tongue, but she respected Michael too much to ask any of them. He'd tell her his story if he wanted to.

From the outside, she'd never be able to tell he had been injured. He walked straight, no visible scars, seeming completely perfect. Then she realized what they had in common. They hid what was really going on inside.

"Did you cook on the field?"

He nodded. "Under a tent, in the middle of Afghanistan."

"Were you afraid?"

"More afraid to leave my mom alone, you know?"

Her eyes moved to his tattoo. The roses a soft pink against his skin.

"She's at Majestic Oaks?" The thought of having her mother there hurt. "It's a nice facility."

He nodded. "Yeah, the staff is great."

"I used to volunteer there."

"Of course, you did."

"Ha, ha." She leaned back on her arms, kicking her feet out. One of the band members checked the mic by tapping it. "Is Loretta still there?"

"Yeah, she's still there." Michael smiled.

"I should go and visit her someday."

"You should come the next time I go."

"I'll do that." She thought about Loretta and how kind she had been to Ally all those years she went to the home, every Wednesday throughout high school.

"Good evening!" a man called into the microphone. "We're the Jack Willow Band, and we're going to start with one of our favorites tonight, called 'She's Mine, Back Off, Man!'"

The crowd hooted and laughed as the lead singer strummed his guitar, with the band in sync. The song's lyrics were comedic, but catchy. After the first few songs, the music became more country and people got up to dance.

Eve and Harry sat silent, she noticed, through the next two songs. She pulled out the box of chocolate truffles she'd brought along and handed it over to them. "I'm going to go to the food tent." She tugged on Michael's shirt. "Michael's coming with me."

"I guess I'm going to the food tent." He rolled his eyes dramatically. "That's exactly what I wanted to do while the band plays."

She pulled on his shirt again and he got up, following her through the crowd, hopping over blankets until they reach the beer tents.

"I want fried clams." She walked toward a food truck with Barnacle Bobby written on the front.

"Fried clams?" He made a face. "Tell me that's not part of the plan."

"I've missed fried seafood." She looked out at the food truck. The same food truck that had been there when she was a little girl.

"Uncle Bobby!"

Michael made a face and asked, "Bobby's your uncle?"

"No."

"Well, well, if it isn't our pride and joy!" Bobby came out of the truck, ignoring the line of customers, and gave her a big hug. "When did you get to town?"

"I came as soon as I heard about the heart attack."

"You're a good daughter." He jabbed his thumb toward the food truck. "Let me get you some clams! I'm going to put an order in now."

Bobby didn't even wait for her to answer, climbing back inside the food truck.

"How are you related to Barnacle Bobby?"

"He's David's best friend from high school. They grew up together and played football on the same team. Even married their high school sweethearts together." Ally paused to let the information sink in. A lot of people forgot that David had married Elise back in the day. When she saw recognition on his face, she continued. "But Bobby's wife died later, and he never remarried, so Frank and David took him in. He's always been another crazy member of the family."

"Who cooks."

"Who cooks."

Michael laughed a little, then studied her "Was it hard?" he asked.

"Was what hard?"

"Being the Princess with two dads?"

She looked up at him and realized how very similar they

were. "Only when I wanted to kick someone's butt when they talked bad about them, but most people only said things behind my back."

Michael nodded. "Me too. No one ever talked about my dad in front of me." He huffed out a laugh. "Not even my mom."

"I can't complain." She couldn't, not with what Michael had been through with his father. She knew the story. He had been on the news. His trial was covered by the local papers. No one stopped talking about it all through high school. She could never complain. "Even with our weird relationship, Frank is a great stepdad who loves me unconditionally, I know that. Plus, have you ever seen a couple more in love?"

Michael smiled. "They really are grossly happy together."

Then an idea flashed in her head. "You should open a pastry themed food truck, by the beach."

"So I can be like Barnacle Bobby?" Michael turned to her and made a face.

"No, I'm serious," she said. "In the morning, people would love it. Plus, it's a lot less overhead and the insurance and rent would be lower."

"I'd have to get a license, and I'd be competing with your dads."

"You don't have to stay in Camden Cove. You could go up to Portland or Kennebunkport. Or go back to school! I bet you could get financial aid and a gig through the school."

"Like you should talk."

"What's that supposed to mean?" she crossed her arms. She was lecturing him, not the other way around.

"You should not be an assistant in a tourist trap."

"It's one of the most well-known patisseries in all of Paris." She couldn't believe he'd call it a tourist trap, even if it *was* a tourist trap.

"With someone else's name." He crossed his own arms.

"*La Patisserie Ally* does not roll off the tongue."

"You don't have to be French, you could just be Ally."

"Easy for you to say, you have a tattoo that'll hook the customers. All I have is a funny American accent and a moped."

"Seriously?" Michael shook his head. "You have a moped?"

"It's what you have in Paris."

"You're good, Ally." He turned serious. "Why do you hold yourself back?"

She opened her mouth to argue, but couldn't think of the reasons. "I've worked hard to get where I am. I'm happy where I am."

Michael rubbed his beard. "Sure. If you say so."

"Seriously, I love my job."

"Okay."

"I do."

"I'm going to hit the restroom." He gave her a salute and walked away.

She nodded and waited, continuing their argument in her head. Grabbing a plastic cup of local IPA, she watched the band from afar. She stood taking in the greasy aroma of fried shellfish, counting down the minutes, when she noticed Michael cutting through the crowd toward her. He stood tall, his broad shoulders doing justice to his t-shirt, and it took everything inside her not to keep ogling. Instead, she looked at his floral tattoo. Suddenly, an image of her wrapping around his waist at Elizabeth's wedding flashed through her head, and her cheeks flushed. He gave her a look as though he'd read her mind. A sly grin that spoke a million words. She took a sip to hide behind her cup, yet she couldn't keep her eyes off him.

Michael hoped she couldn't read his mind, because she'd be blushing even more if she knew what he was thinking. Something about Ally pulled him in, and not just her beauty. He liked her quick wit and dry sense of humor. She was one of the few who actually seemed to get him. His quiet demeanor put a lot of women off. Not Ally. If anything, it encouraged her to talk. In the kitchen, if he stayed silent, she'd either talk whether he responded or not, or carried on quietly by herself. But she didn't need to fill the space with conversation, either, just because they were together. Recently though, he always had something to talk to her about. In fact, more and more, he looked forward to talking to her. Hearing what she had to say about anything and everything. What he most looked forward to was watching her bake. Watching Ally do her thing in the kitchen had changed him. He didn't want to be that guy doing something he *kind of* wanted to do. Ally showed him he didn't have to stop dreaming big, just because he was living in Camden Cove.

That was probably why it surprised him that she was so insecure, because she wasn't at all insecure in the kitchen. Ally was holding herself back in Paris for a guy named Jean-Paul, not because of a lack of ability.

His musings were cut short when Bobby brought out fresh fried clam strips with plenty of tartar sauce.

"How are your fried clams?" he asked, as they walked back to Harry and Eve, who from afar seemed to be happily enjoying themselves.

"Heaven." She dipped another clam in the tartar sauce. "I haven't had these in so long."

"You eat salad for breakfast, and dream of fried clams." He shot a glance at her, almost said something else, then changed his mind.

"What?"

He shook his head. "It's nothing."

"You were about to rip on me, I'm sure. What is it?"

He shook his head. "No, I was going to tell you I'm having a really nice time tonight."

She held onto a fried clam and said, "Oh."

He shrugged. "I mean, when you're not complaining."

"Ha, ha." She took a bite of her clam, looking at the pile of fried food instead of him, and said, "Me, too. I'm having a nice time."

They stood there, the music from the band failing to fill the awkward silence between them.

"Should we go back?"

"Yeah, sure."

She led the way to the blanket and shared her box of clams and fries with Eve and Harry.

"I love Barnacle Bobby's clams," Harry said, raising an eyebrow at the two.

Ally started talking to Eve about Paris, but Michael just observed the situation from his side of the blanket. He liked Ally. A lot. Which was dangerous. She certainly wasn't going to leave Jean-Paul for a line cook in Camden Cove. And he couldn't leave his mother. Having a thing for Ally Williams was a suicide mission. What was he thinking?

By the end of the last set, Harry and Eve had set up a dinner at The Fish Market. Ally had made their reservation, calling her cousin's restaurant herself and getting them the loft seating. The best spot in the house, overlooking the ocean.

They picked up their stuff and began folding the blankets. Ally stumbled forward, almost falling, when someone bumped into her, and looked up to see Todd Brewer, a local fisherman, who had clearly hit the beer tent one too many times. Ally pushed him off her, but stumbled back, before Michael grabbed her.

"What do you think you're doing, man?" Michael said, pushing Brewer away. He turned to Ally. "Are you okay?"

"Tell your woman here to watch out where she's walking."

"Keep walking, Brewer," Michael ordered.

Brewer pointed a finger. "Aren't you Mikey's boy?"

"Get your finger out of my face, Brewer," Michael advised the man. He thrust his chest out.

"Isn't your Daddy still in prison?"

Harry joined them, maneuvering himself between the two men. "Michael, ignore him. He's drunk."

Michael could feel his anger growing. He tried to control it, holding it down, pushing it away as hard as he could.

Brewer smiled when he saw Michael's fist clench up. "Wasn't your mom the town whore?" Brewer stepped closer to Ally. "I bet this one's fun in the sack."

Michael swung at Brewer and hit him smack in the jaw. The man stumbled back, grabbing his face. Then he charged like a bull at Michael and Harry. Michael pushed Harry out of the way as the overweight, burly man rammed his body into him. He felt the switch inside, like a light turning on, all those years of training shooting to the surface, turning him into a soldier again.

He stood in a fighting stance, ready for whatever came next. The man rammed into him, but Michael pushed him to the ground. Brewer fell on his knees but wasn't deterred, if anything he was more incensed. He leaped up and ran his shoulder into Michael's stomach, and this time Michael pushed him down harder. Brewer was no match for him. A crowd began to gather.

"Why don't you give it a rest, man, before you get hurt."

Brewer spat on the ground and charged again, scratching at Michael, flailing his arms like a child, but Michael held him back, knocking him down for the third time. A couple of bystanders grabbed the man, and he seemed to run out of steam. Through the crowd, he could see Officer Paulson pushing his way toward them. The same old officer from when he got in trouble in high school.

Michael pulled out his keys and handed them to Harry. "Looks like you're going to have to drive the women home tonight."

"Michael Mailloux, don't move!" Paulson yelled out. "Stay right where you are!"

Harry froze as though the officer was talking to him. Brewer moaned, rubbing his jaw. Michael shook out his hand while the overweight police officer arrived on the scene.

"You're coming with me."

"Why?"

"I saw you physically assault a man." Paulson didn't even take notice of the slurs Brewer was spewing.

"Are you kidding me?" Michael thrusted his hand toward the man, and Paulson grabbed it and pulled it behind his back, slapping cuffs around his wrist.

"You have the right to remain silent," Officer Paulson rambled off Michael's rights as he cuffed him.

"Excuse me!" Ally yelled. "You can't arrest this man!"

"I can arrest whoever I want, now back off, ma'am." He tightened the cuffs.

"Did you call me ma'am?" Ally's face wrinkled in disgust. "He was protecting me from that drunk."

"He punched a man in the face and continually pushed him to the ground, *ma'am*."

"Ma'am?!" Ally's face reddened. "I'm calling my lawyer."

"You do that, because Michael might just need one."

"You can't do this."

"Ally, stop," Michael said. "Don't make this a bigger deal than it has to be."

"Get out of the way, *ma'am*." Paulson took Michael's other hand.

Michael didn't fight him. It wasn't worth arguing with a man who was already getting too much enjoyment out of the situation.

"Can you meet me at the station?" Ally said into her phone.

"Ally, stop," Michael said, as Paulson escorted him through the crowd toward his squad car.

"I'm calling Chief Martinez, next!" she shouted.

"Good luck. He's out of town, fishing with your cousins."

"Ally, go home, I'm fine." Michael couldn't look at her. He didn't want to see her look at him the way she did. What the heck was he thinking, punching Brewer? He shook his head as they headed toward the SUV.

"Get in."

Michael ducked his head as he sat down, his hands now throbbing as the circulation was cut off.

Ally ran up to the car before the door was closed. "Elizabeth's husband Adam is going to meet us at the police station."

"Go home, Ally."

"No, I won't let you get charged with anything because of me."

"Go home," Paulson said as he slammed the door.

"Are you going to arrest Brewer?!" she yelled through the glass. "*You* ma'am, are going to be arrested next, if you don't stop yelling at an officer of the law."

Harry stood in front of Ally and gently pushed her away from the officer. "Don't worry, Michael, we're coming."

Michael rested his head against the front seat, wishing he could be bringing Ally home, instead of heading to the police station.

CHAPTER 10

*J*ean-Paul called three times while Harry drove Eve home, then headed to the station. Each time, Ally turned the ringer off and let it go to voicemail. She couldn't talk now. Not when Michael had been arrested for standing up to that jerk for her.

Adam waited on the steps of the station as she and Harry pulled up.

"He's inside." Adam stood in front of her. "But he doesn't want you here. He wants you to go home."

"He can want me to go home all he wants, but I'm here to give my statement about what happened."

Adam shook his head. "It looks like no one is pressing charges, and Michael will be released once everything is cleared."

"I want to press charges!" Ally couldn't believe no one took that guy seriously. "That man was drunk and disorderly."

"Ally, the officer said he witnessed the whole thing, and Michael swung first."

"That's because that guy was obnoxious."

Adam held up his hands. "Look, this is the best-case scenario right now for Michael, because he *did* hit the guy."

"Oh."

"I'll bring you home, and come back to make sure he's okay."

"No, I'm not leaving until I know he's going to get out."

Adam sighed. "Ally, please, he doesn't want you here."

Harry took out the keys to Michael's truck. "I can bring her home."

Adam nodded. "Thanks. I'll stay here and make sure everything works out."

Ally felt defeated. "Fine, but you'll call me when he gets out, right?"

Adam nodded. "Go. He's just going through processing, then I'll bring him home."

Harry walked to Michael's truck and started the engine without saying a word. Ally couldn't even think straight.

"I feel terrible." She bit her thumbnail.

"Look." Harry threw the shift into drive. "Michael doesn't have a lot of people in his life he can count on. I think he's beginning to like you, you know, and I don't want to see him get hurt." Harry pushed his glasses up his nose.

She had never really thought about it like that.

"I'm not saying he *does* like you, because Michael is not the kind of guy who would sit in a truck talking about who he likes with anyone, but he's different around you. He's totally different."

"What do you mean?"

"Like, he went out in public. He sat on a blanket, listening to a band with other people."

"What are you saying, he doesn't leave the house?"

"Not really, no." Harry blew out. "Not since coming back from Afghanistan."

Ally's heart sank.

"He works, visits his mom, and buys books. He'll fit in time for a poker game here and there, but I haven't seen him out, like tonight, since high school."

"Oh."

"Look, just make sure you don't lead him in the wrong direction, if you know what I mean?"

Her shoulders fell. "Of course. I wasn't trying to…"

He held up his hand. "I know you're not trying to lead him on, all I'm saying is, be careful."

"I will."

~

Adam Cahill was a decent man, Michael realized, as he sat in the police station. Obviously, this wasn't the usual kind of law he practiced, but he performed like a powerhouse, frightening everyone with his command of the law. Adam scared Paulson so much, he didn't even press charges after Brewer passed out. Witnesses told the story of a drunk Brewer falling on top of Ally Williams and Michael stepping in.

"It should at least be a disorderly conduct," the officer grunted at Adam.

"You have no proof but your own biased account of what happened." Adam had deduced that Paulson hadn't even seen the punch, but heard it from someone in the crowd.

"You've got to be kidding me?" Officer Paulson had met his match.

When Alex Martinez called Adam back, it was no contest. Paulson let him go.

Michael had wanted to do more than swing an uppercut. Brewer deserved it. In the end though, Michael felt bad for the poor guy. He wasn't much different than Michael himself, apart from the drinking. All alone, with no one at home.

"Brewer. Let us take you home."

He sat up, squinting. "I don't need a ride." His middle finger jabbed up before he flopped down in his cot.

Adam drove him home, and after Michael got out of the truck, he leaned back in. "I can pay you for tonight. I know you were doing a favor for Ally, but I can pay."

Adam shook his head. "No, really. I can't stand Paulson, so whenever I can give him a hard time, I enjoy myself."

"I don't need a handout."

"Honestly, what you're doing for Ally and her dads is enough." He waved Michael off. "I'll see you around."

"Yeah, man, thanks again." He patted the truck's hood as he stepped away.

Adam nodded as he reversed out of the driveway. Michael faced his childhood home. An old New Englander was what people called it. A basic two story, two bedroom, one and a half bath, with the kitchen in the back. The porch was the best part.

He climbed up the steps, wishing he'd just stayed home. He could've sat out there and read until the light from the evening sun disappeared. But he wouldn't have been with Ally.

He had grown up in the house, never lived anywhere else except when in the military. He never missed living in Camden Cove when he was away. He hadn't really had any desire to come back, and he'd sell the house as soon as his mother... He let out a sigh as he unlocked the front door.

Heading into the kitchen, he flipped on the lights before grabbing a glass from the dish rack. His hands shook, and he slowly squeezed his swollen knuckles as he held the glass under the faucet. Letting out a deep breath, he gripped the countertop, squeezing to control his emotions. This was when he wanted to drink. To stop the inevitable pain. To stop the flashbacks. To stop the anxiety crawling under his skin. To stop the waking nightmares that plagued him.

His leg burned. It pulsed as though the bombing had happened only yesterday. The familiar ringing filled his ears as he sat down at the kitchen table, no longer in Camden Cove, but somewhere very far away.

~

Ally lay in her childhood bed, staring at the ceiling, replaying the night. Had she been leading Michael on? Here she was, about to turn thirty for God's sake, and she was still staring at the ceiling trying to figure out the opposite sex. How many nights had she done this in high school? All those broken hearts.

This time it wasn't about her heart, although that hurt, too. She didn't want to break something she never knew existed, and was now afraid she had already lost. Why did life have to get even more complicated?

She had her dream life in Paris.

Camden Cove was the place she'd wanted to leave since the day she moved there as a little girl. Always wanting to go back to Paris, the magical City of Light. Of music. Of art. Of culture. Of fashion. Of food as an art form. A thing of beauty.

Paris bloomed with beauty in everything, even in Ally. She felt lighter and sweeter when speaking in French. She understood their pace of life and enjoyed their way of living. She had even thought of applying for citizenship. She loved her family, but she didn't belong in Camden Cove.

And she loved Jean-Paul.

So, why couldn't she stop thinking of Michael?

She turned on her bedroom light and opened the closet. Switching on the lights, the walk-in closet was illuminated before her. It was filled mostly with her mother and Martin's clothes, but she saw what she was looking for on the top shelf. Her yearbooks.

She started with senior year, flipping right to the M section. Michael Mailloux.

He wasn't there. She flipped the pages to see if she'd missed something, but he wasn't even listed. Then she grabbed the junior year volume, and there he was. The small black and white photo. He had a longer, unkempt haircut. Same grin. She could tell that posing for the photo had killed him. He was just as handsome, but she didn't remember ever thinking about him like that, back then. Probably because the football players stole her attention.

She sat down on the carpet and studied his eyes. The fact was, they had a lot in common. Well, they had cooking, and they had a past that wouldn't leave them alone. But since she came back to Camden Cove, he had turned into someone she enjoyed being around. He was funny and seemed to enjoy picking on her quirky insecurities, but also ignited something inside her that she hadn't even known was there.

Michael made her want to be better in all things. She was even reading those stupid books he gave her. He pushed her out of her comfort zone, and now she had ideas, new concepts and thoughts, new recipes she wanted to try with him. Things she couldn't do in Paris.

Things she didn't do with Jean-Paul.

Michael understood baking like she did.

Michael understood her. He got her, where most of the people in her life at this moment did not. Not her fathers, not her mother, not even Martin. Elizabeth? Maybe, but she had a new life, a new family. In Paris, her friends were people she met through Jean-Paul. And if she was really honest with herself, Michael got her better than Jean-Paul did.

She looked at her phone and reread Jean-Paul's texts. He missed her. He loved her. He wanted her to come back. He told her to call, but she decided to text.

I'll call tomorrow. Miss you, too, she wrote, but as she set the phone on her dresser, she decided to send another text but to Michael.

You okay?

She kept checking to see if he was reading it, but the screen remained blank. The message had been delivered. But by the time she finally fell asleep, Michael still hadn't replied.

When she woke, she immediately checked her phone. Nothing. She flung off her covers and got dressed, slipped her feet into a pair of flip-flops, and stole her Mom's car. It was still dark as she drove toward Michael's house, not a single creature stirring... except for Michael. When she pulled into his driveway, she saw him rocking in a chair on his porch.

"Hey," she whispered, walking slowly up the steps.

"Hey."

He stood up and walked to the front door, gesturing for her to come inside. His house looked lived in, not like the minimalist affair she imagined. She looked around, catching photographs of Michael through the years, standing with family as a little boy. Then she realized that this was his mother's house. The house he grew up in. A crocheted blanket hung on the wall, floral curtains covered the windows, and framed biblical quotes sat on the side tables next to the couch. There was nothing that indicated he was staying there, certainly not living there.

"What are you doing here, Ally?" He sounded exhausted.

She squeezed her hands together. "I am so sorry about last night. That guy was a jerk, and you stood up for me, and then got arrested, and it's entirely my fault."

"Ally." He didn't let her continue. "None of it was your fault."

"I feel really bad." She looked away.

He let out a breath. "You don't have to feel bad."

"You wouldn't have gotten in trouble if I didn't fuss about the guy—"

"Ally," he interrupted. "Please, it's fine."

She closed her mouth, squeezing her hands together, thinking of what to say next. He stood with his arms crossed, his chest puffed out. She couldn't read him as he stood quietly in his mother's living room. Then she saw his hand, swollen and discolored. She reached out without thinking. "You should put some ice on it."

He didn't move, but he also didn't pull his hand away. "Ally, what are you doing here?"

She looked up at him, his eyes intense and mysterious, yet she felt safe. She looked back at his hand. "Thank you for standing up for me."

She glanced back up, her body flushed with heat as he slowly leaned closer to her, his lips so close she could feel his breath on hers. And just as he was about to kiss her she shouted, "I can't!"

He stopped, pulled his hand out of her grasp, and took a step back.

Her heart dropped. Why did she have to yell it out? She just didn't want things to get even more complicated than they were. Michael was someone she really liked.

"Ally," he said coldly. "You should go."

CHAPTER 11

"Stop following me around like a puppy," David said to Frank as they walked around the kitchen. "Who organized this place? Didn't they see I already have a system?"

"You mean the system only you understood?" Frank shook his head. "Ally did all of it, and it's great. I can finally find things."

"Ally, you did all of this?" David turned toward her.

She just shrugged.

"Yes," Frank said, ushering David through the kitchen. "She's been so helpful."

"I guess I could live with this." David picked through his pantry, checking the new containers Ally had picked up. "You're so traditional."

"Sorry?" she swiveled on the stool, picking at a piece of dried flour on the countertop.

"You've become quite the chef," Frank said.

"Well, she always had been." David turned back to the kitchen and took a seat, already exhausted. He took in a deep breath and held it in before letting go. "Do you think we should ask?"

"Ask me what?" Ally looked back and forth between the two, carrying on a conversation as if she wasn't there.

Frank nodded. "It's time, David."

"I just don't want her to think she has to say yes to make us happy." She could see David's emotions taking over. "This pain medication is making me loopy." He dabbed his eyes with a handkerchief. "You said Michael's doing great?"

"Ask me what?" Ally said louder, standing.

"It's time." Frank rubbed his hand along the counter.

"Hello!" Ally said. "I'm right here."

"What's up with you?" Frank asked.

"What?"

"You look terrible," David said.

She looked at Frank, then back at him. "Sorry, but are you feeling well?"

"I'm fine."

"Then what's bothering you?"

"You two were literally just talking about me as though I'm not here." Ally rolled her eyes. "What do you guys need to talk about?"

"Your dad wants to retire," Frank burst out.

Ally's eyes widened and she turned to David. "What?"

"Don't worry, I'm fine, we'll be okay."

"We'd like to offer the bakery to you."

"What?" Ally sat down on the stool. "You want to give it to me?"

"Well, who else?"

"Um... I don't know, anyone else in town?"

"Ally, stop being so dramatic." David rolled his eyes at his daughter. "We think you'd be great, but we completely understand if you want to pass, and continue working in Paris."

"Oh."

"We can run things on the sidelines for the time being, and give the responsibilities to another chef."

"Like who?" she snapped. "You'd offer it to Michael, right?"

Frank looked at David, giving him the *told you so* look.

"Yes."

She nodded, looking out the window. "I have to think about this."

"Of course."

"I mean, you never talked about retiring, and stuff."

"I never had a heart attack before." David let out a long sigh. "I know we haven't been very supportive about you being with Jean-Paul, and this is not to get you to move back. We want you to be happy, and if that's in Paris, then we don't want to stop you. But maybe you and Jean-Paul would want to run La Patisserie in Camden Cove instead of staying in Paris."

She couldn't believe what was happening. She could have her own bakery.

Or Michael could get his dream job.

Then there was Jean-Paul, and her life in Paris. "When do you need a decision?"

David shrugged, then looked to Frank. "We're happy to wait as long as you need."

She nodded, but she knew that keeping them waiting wasn't fair. They needed to know soon. "I would have to talk to Jean-Paul."

"Yes, well, we figured."

"I can't believe you're offering me the bakery."

"We believe you'd do great things with this place." Frank wrapped his arms around her. "We're sorry we haven't shown it, but we believe in you."

Michael had never been more thankful to be off work. He couldn't face Ally today. Not after last night. He couldn't even believe he let himself think there might be something in the way she looked at him, other than as a friend. He laughed at his ridiculousness. Ally was the top shelf, while he was the gutter.

He pulled into Majestic Oaks later than usual. He hadn't slept the night before. All he thought about was Ally.

He looked out the windshield at the nursing home. The brick building looked like no home. It looked like a business, sterile and uninviting. This was where he'd spend his holidays, his birthday, his mother's birthday, and Loretta's. This was where he'd spend every weekend and mid-week evening. He'd have to be okay. This was it for him.

He pushed open his door and jumped out. He'd stay for just a few minutes today, not sure how he'd be able to take the constant questions or the fear in her eyes when he told her the truth.

The sliding doors shushed open and he walked down the corridor. He could already hear Loretta's voice from the nursing station as he stepped into the Alzheimer's Unit. Another voice spoke, and he immediately recognized it.

When he turned the corner, there she was, sitting with Loretta.

"Ally, what are you doing here?"

She smiled and stood. His shoulders tensed.

Loretta's eyes slid over to him. "I didn't know you knew our Ms. Ally."

Michael straightened his posture. "I work over at her dads' place now."

"Small world." Loretta fisted her hands on her hips. "Well, your mom's out in the rec room, over by the windows. She's quiet today."

Michael nodded, biting his bottom lip. Quiet was better for him. The whole Ally thing completely threw him off, and he really didn't know how he felt about her showing up here. His head was way too messed up from the night before.

"I better go check on Joan. Her feet were bothering her this morning." Loretta grabbed a clipboard and walked away, leaving Ally and him alone.

"I brought some books." Ally held out a bag. He could see familiar titles. She must've gone to Harry's place, or thought he enjoyed large print romance. "I remembered when you bought some titles for your mom at the bookstore."

"How'd you know I'd be here?"

She placed the bag on the floor when he didn't take it. "I called Loretta and asked her when you usually came in. I took a chance you'd stick to the predictable routine."

"What do you want, Ally?"

"I want to say I'm sorry." Dark circles ringed her eyes.

"What for? You have a boyfriend." He picked up the bag. "Thanks for the books."

"I'm sorry if I led you on."

"No need." He shook his head. He wanted this over as soon as possible.

"It's just that my life in Paris with Jean-"

"Paul, right, I know." He turned to leave. "Thanks again for the books."

"Stop, Michael." She grabbed for his arm, but he stepped out of her reach.

"Stop what, Ally? I get it. You have a completely different life back in Paris that's just been interrupted. I shouldn't have thought the way you were acting meant anything."

"I'm sorry."

He stood there, tapping his thumb against his leg. "Why do you feel like everyone has to like you?"

"What?"

"You can't pass a stranger without making sure they love you by the time you leave."

"That's not true."

"Then why this, Princess?" He gestured between them.

"I am not a princess." Her eyes narrowed. "I thought you were my friend."

"Look, Ally, if you need a friend, I'm not really the guy for that."

"I don't need just any friend."

He made a face. "Well, then you'll need to figure that out for yourself."

Tears came to the surface of her eyelids.

He had to look away, hoping Loretta didn't hear anything. Ally walked past him, down the corridor to the exit. He didn't turn around. He couldn't. He didn't want to feel anymore. He wanted things to go back to the way they were before Ally Williams came to town. Back to the stable routine he had grown accustomed to. Back to being numb.

～

Ally sat out on the beach, in the sand, looking out at the horizon. She watched the seagulls float on the water, the evening sun warming her back. She rested her head on arms that wrapped around her knees. So much had happened since she returned home.

She still hadn't called Jean-Paul back, and she didn't know what she'd say if she did. If she told him about the bakery, would he beg her to stay in Paris? Would he think about coming to Maine? She had a feeling he wouldn't, which made her ask why *she* stayed in Paris. Working at La Patisserie showed her that she wasn't happy with what she was doing at Jean-Paul's bakery. She had no control over any of her work. She was basically just another employee, easily replaced.

Would he be okay if she decided to stay? He certainly wasn't going to leave Paris for Camden Cove. There were plenty of pastry chefs lined up behind her. Was she, as a girlfriend, as easily replaced?

Then there was Michael.

Before he arrived, Loretta had told her about his mother, about her disease, about how he had placed her there in the nursing home after six years of taking care of her. How he came to see her almost every day. And how he held her hand when she was scared.

The look on his face when he saw her at the nursing home had been unmistakable. It was the same look on his face the day at the hospital when she first insulted him, a look of disdain.

She had never felt so horrible in her life.

The tide had moved out from the beach, leaving puddles that reflected the pinking sky above. Lights from inside the shops and cottages lit up the edge of the coast as the pinks faded into black at the earth's edge. Her life across the ocean was in the dark.

There was nothing left in Camden Cove for her. Her dad was getting better every day. Michael clearly didn't need her help. They had hired someone to take over Kate's duties, which meant she didn't have to help work the counter with Frank. Her mom and Martin were living happily as empty nesters. Elizabeth had a new wonderful life of her own.

When the sun had completely faded away and the stars twinkled above, she walked to her dads' place. They lived only a few blocks away from the beach. She climbed the formal entrance steps she had never used as a kid, and rang the doorbell. When Frank answered the door, she didn't wait to speak.

"I made my decision."

CHAPTER 12

*A*lly sat at Elizabeth's kitchen table as she waited for the coffee to brew. Elizabeth's belly already stuck out further than the last time she'd seen her. "You look extra pregnant today."

"That's because I finished off a half gallon of Toasted Almond Fudge for breakfast." Elizabeth rubbed her belly. "I'm pretty sure I'm carrying a linebacker."

Ally couldn't help feeling a pang of jealousy. She had been at Elizabeth's through their morning routine, watching them get ready together. Lucy fed and watered the animals. Elizabeth helped. Adam made breakfast while listening to the news on NPR, Lucy complaining about how boring it was.

"He's going to be okay, right?" She asked him about Michael for the fifth time.

"Yes. The officer in question is Paulson, who has a history with Michael."

"What's their history?"

"He was his probation officer as a teenager."

"Remember how he got caught stealing? He's the one who was involved with Michael's father's arrest," Elizabeth said.

Ally wondered what his father had really done to be imprisoned all these years. She had heard the town gossip. The story was that he'd stolen a lot of money from a lot of people in town. But it felt wrong to ask, as though she was invading Michael's privacy. Ally thought about the happy photographs in Michael's house. She wondered if that was before his father went to prison.

Ally thought about the rumors throughout high school. Then about what she had said about him that night in the hospital. Elise was right. Ally had judged him, and she hated herself even more.

"You don't mind taking me to the airport?" she asked Adam. She wanted to leave as soon as she could. Frank was taking her dad to a doctor's appointment, and her mom and Martin had a tee time for golf which she'd told them to keep.

He shook his head. "Lucy and I wanted to go see the city. It'll be a nice day in Boston."

Elizabeth handed Ally her coffee and gave her a big hug, rubbing her back. "I'm going to miss you!"

Ally smiled. "Yeah, it's been nice seeing everyone again. I'll be back when the baby arrives."

She wondered if Elizabeth saw through her lie.

The whole ride to the airport, she sat quietly as Lucy filled her in on all the details of an imagined trip to Paris. Lucy wanted to go to all the museums, especially the Louvre. She also wanted to go to the countryside and ride horses. Ally nodded and smiled at the appropriate times, but her mind was elsewhere.

When they reached the airport, she grabbed her things.

Lucy ran into her arms. "Bon voyage, Tante Ally!"

"Bon voyage, ma belle niece, Lucy!"

She turned to Adam and gave him a big hug. "Thank you so much for everything."

"No problem, it's been nice catching up."

"Let me know as soon as Elizabeth goes into labor."

"I will." He put his arm around Lucy. "Lucy will make sure of it."

Lucy waved as she got back into the truck. Ally stood waving back as they drove off, leaving her at the departures gate of Logan Airport, alone.

~

When Michael opened the bakery that morning, he half-expected, half-hoped to see Ally in the kitchen, but only an empty silence greeted him. He flipped all the lights on and began the prep work, pulling out baking sheets filled with pastries ready for the ovens. By the time the morning staff showed up to open, however, Michael had lost his focus. He could only rehash how he had treated Ally in the nursing home.

Cruddy.

That was how he'd treated her, and the fact that she didn't show up this morning told him how she felt.

Cruddy.

He pulled out his phone, about to text an apology, but changed his mind, stuffing it back into his pocket. There was no use apologizing. She didn't need a guy like him bothering her. He was Michael Mailloux junior, the son of a crook, a man who lived in his mother's house, with no real future.

By midday, he itched to go home. He was unable to concentrate on any one task for long before his mind wandered back to Ally. When David and Frank came into the bakery, he immediately untied his apron, ready to bolt, but David asked if they could talk.

Had they found out about his arrest? Were they ready to come back, and telling him to go back to The Fish Market?

"We wanted to talk to you about working here permanently."

He jerked his head back. "Work here… permanently?"

"Yes, well, the heart attack showed us we need to slow down, and Ally just spoke the world of your abilities as a chef," David said. "We will still run the business side of things. But I can't bake *and* run the business anymore."

Michael couldn't believe it. This was a dream come true, but running a kitchen wasn't only *his* dream. "What about Ally? Did you ask her?"

Frank nodded. "She suggested you when she turned us down."

His heart fell. "She did?"

"So, what do you think?"

He shook his head. His whole world had changed within minutes. "Of course, I'll take it."

Frank smiled at David. "Great."

"Are you sure Ally doesn't want it?" He knew how good she was at running that kitchen herself, even the cooking classes. This was her gig, not his.

David shook his head. "She's already flown back to Paris. Her life is over there."

Michael's mouth immediately went dry. "She left?"

Frank handed him a rolled-up magazine tied with a ribbon and a note. "She gave us this to give to you."

Michael took it, untied the ribbon, and pulled out the note. The *Madame* magazine was all in French, but the note was in her handwriting.

You always have a place to stay if you come to Paris. Love, Ally.

Ally laid her head against the window, looking out at the dark sea. She'd had a quick layover in Iceland, and now she was only an hour away from Paris, from Jean-Paul, from her old life. Jean-Paul said he'd be waiting for her at the luggage carousel. She wondered what he thought of her coming back.

The sun had begun to set as the plane glided through the clouds, descending on the city. The whole landscaped twinkled, the Seine like a vein running through the heart of Paris. Paris never disappointed. Her stomach swirled with nerves, but she reminded herself this was her home. Michael would never leave his mom for her. Plus, now he had his dream job.

When the wheels touched down, she turned on her phone,

scrolling through the texts looking for his name, but there was nothing from Michael. Nothing at all.

She blew out a deep breath, fogging up the window as the plane taxied to the terminal. The lights from inside the airport showed people scurrying about, running to a flight or walking down the airport with a bag trailing behind. Jean-Paul would already have arrived, and be waiting by the baggage claim.

This was where she belonged.

She climbed out of her seat when the line started moving, going through the motions. Her heart raced with the thought of seeing Jean-Paul. She headed down the red hallway of Paris-Charles-de-Gaulle Airport. Customs went smoothly, and when she stepped through, she saw him there in a small crowd, waiting.

"You grew a beard," was the first thing that came out of her mouth. She almost didn't recognize him.

"Oui, do you like it?"

She thought of Michael's beard. Jean-Paul reached out and kissed her, holding her in his arms. She was stiff and hard to hold, but he didn't stop. He hugged her tighter, then nestled his face in her hair. He smelled different.

"How was your flight?" He wrapped his arm around her waist and steered her toward the bags.

"Fine, it was fine."

Surprisingly, the whole trip back ended up being a breeze. Her luggage was the first to come out, and they quickly grabbed a taxi. Traffic was light on the *Autoroutes*. The driver wound through the city, quiet even for a weekday. Jean-Paul held her hand and kissed it as she looked out the window.

"How is your father?"

"Fine. He's fine."

"Tres bien."

Her eyes never left the window, but all she saw were images from the last month of her life.

"You must be exhausted from all the travel."

She nodded. It was true, since she hadn't slept in almost two days. Not because of the travel, but because of her broken heart. How could she have a broken heart over someone she'd never had? "I'd like to get some sleep."

Once inside her apartment, Jean-Paul brought her bags into her bedroom. She grabbed a glass of water and gulped down half of it before setting the glass on the counter.

"Do you have me on the schedule, tomorrow?" she asked. She wasn't going to be able to sit around the apartment doing nothing but live in her head.

"Well, I had to move you around, now that your back," he said.

Something about the way he said it made her stop and think. "Did you hire someone?"

"Well, you have been gone for almost a month, Ally." He flung his hand out defensively. "What was I supposed to do?"

"You told me it would be alright."

"Yes, but don't expect that just because you're my girlfriend, you get special privileges. That's not fair for those that worked extra shifts because you went home."

"My dad had a heart attack." She couldn't believe him. She could feel her face redden, anger building up. "I wasn't on vacation, and you told me it would be fine to go."

"It was fine." His face softened. He walked over to her, grabbing her hands and kissing her. "Tout ira bien. Everything will be fine."

"I'm going to take a shower and go to bed."

"Oui," he said. "Come to the patisserie tomorrow and we can get you on the schedule."

"Merci," she said, surrendering her anger toward him. "Sorry, it's just been a long few days."

She almost told him about the bakery, but stopped herself. What did it matter now, anyways? She had made her decision, and she'd have to live with it.

After Jean-Paul left, she closed her bedroom and pulled out

her phone. She looked down at Michael's last text message. She fell onto the bed, reading the words over and over again.

She missed him.

CHAPTER 13

*A*lly pulled on her white chef's jacket with her name embroidered in black on the chest. When she first arrived at La Patisserie Michalak, even though her French had been horrible, most of the staff didn't seem to mind filling in the words she was missing. Over time her vocabulary grew, and she could get around the busy kitchen just fine.

Soon she started shopping the markets, finding fresh ingredients, becoming a regular. Her station in the kitchen was tartes, and she made each one with seasonal produce. It was how she won Jean-Paul over in the first place, in Quebec. She had been a pastry chef at a little bistro in Montreal. Jean-Paul asked his server for the name of the chef who baked the tarte. She came out of the kitchen, flattered that someone recognized her talents. She stopped dead in her tracks when she saw the handsome man speaking French in full stream. She had only been in Montreal for a little under a year, and most people spoke English to her. She caught the first words.

"Vous avez beaucoup de talent." He began, his hands swinging around in circles as he spoke. "Tu dois travailler pour moi."

She didn't know where he was from or where the job was that he was offering her, but she didn't care. "Oui."

"Ce serait mervelleux."

He took her out to dinner the next night and told her all about the patisserie he ran in Paris. That night still rang magically in her mind. She thought her dreams had come true, but as she stood in the kitchen of Jean-Paul's patisserie, the heart of the bustling machine of pastries, it no longer felt like a dream.

At her station, she went through the motions. The young chef Jean-Paul had hired while she was away had been moved to the towering of the *divins*. He seemed less than pleased with her return. Her friend Margot greeted her when she arrived, but the rest of the staff seemed cooler than usual. She didn't care. She didn't even bother to ask how the time had gone while she was away, because she already knew. It had been the same for the past two years.

"Tell me you're going out with us tonight?" Margot asked. "Have you seen the new girl? She's a model, from the south, named Claudia."

She hadn't heard of this new hire, Claudia. But her ears perked up when she heard a woman's giggle in Jean-Paul's office when she returned from the pantry. She slipped around the corner and saw him sitting on his desk next to a woman whose legs seemed endless. She wore the black and white uniform, but it fit like it was made for her. Not frumpy, like on the rest of the women out front.

Claudia whipped her hair to one side and smiled at her. She stood up and walked out in four-inch heels, sashaying out to the floor.

"She's very pretty," Ally noted, now watching Jean-Paul, who turned toward his desk, shuffling papers.

"Oui, she's tres belle."

"Ah."

As soon as she walked into his office, Jean-Paul dropped the papers and took her hand. He had never been one for romantic gestures, which seemed ironic since he was French. "Tonight, let me take you out for dinner. We can go to Le Basilic."

"The place we went on our anniversary?" she asked. She did enjoy the charming restaurant. "Qui sonne tres bein."

But she didn't look forward to it. After her shift she walked home, taking the long way to Square Louise-Michel and climbing the hill to the steps of the Sacre-Coeur Basilica. Its creamy domes towering over her still made her feel the way she had when she was a little girl. A beautiful insignificance. To think how many others through the history of the world had come to these very steps to find answers to their problems. Her issues were hardly even worth bringing to this sacred space.

Tourists filed in and out of the basilica, photographing everything around them. She remembered feeling the same way when she first came as an adult with Jean-Paul, unable to take in the enormity of the structure and the view of the city. She headed to her spot, the place her parents used to take her as a little girl, along the fountain's walls, and looked out. Here, at the highest point in Paris, Ally could see the entire city, but her excitement had dwindled to a faint blip.

The bells rang out. The sound vibrated through her chest and the familiar song pricked tears behind her eyes. She wished more than anything she could have Michael sitting next to her. She'd point out the Eifel tower and the statue of Joan of Arc. She'd take him inside to see the dome and the neo-byzantine painting of Jesus. She'd buy him a book of the history, then take him to the tiny patisserie down the road called *La Gouette d'Or*, her favorite patisserie in the city. She'd take them the long way back through the side streets near the cemetery, then back around again at night to see the dome lit up from below.

She shook her head, reminding herself that her home was in Paris, and Michael's was in Camden Cove.

Michael stood outside his mother's home, pushing the lawnmower along the side of the house. He kept staring at the place where he grew up. It didn't mean much anymore, now that his mom had moved out. At one point it was his safe haven, but after his mother got sick, it became a mausoleum, a place where everything that was good and true in his previous life was held, but only on display.

He cut the mower, still staring at the house. It was like it had frozen in time. If he could go back ten years, he'd probably be doing the same exact thing. Some chore for his mother, some-thing to make her happy, but she was never the same after his father left. She drank frequently but she was no drunk, just sad, desperate not to feel the pain of losing someone she loved. Losing a life she loved. She did the best she could with what she had.

He dragged the mower back to the shed and climbed up the back steps. He pulled off his sneakers and threw them down at the bottom of the steps. His hands were dirty, so he wiped his brow with his arm and looked out toward the east. During quiet, clear nights in the winter, he could hear the waves, but the leaves of the trees muffled the waves in the summer.

It was hard to keep his mind off her, but hard to imagine what she was doing.

Last night, he broke and looked up her address, and the patis-serie, and Jean-Paul. A dream life, for sure. She lived in the heart of Paris on a trendy street, according to a trip advisor website. La Patisserie Michalak sat near the basilica at the top of Paris, a pris-tine shop with dozens of beautiful delicacies for the tourists. Jean-Paul had the most pictures when you googled any of the three options. His apartment had been photographed for a Parisian magazine. In most of the images of the bakery, he stood leaning against something — a counter, the stove, a window. He was also connected with many well-to-do people in Paris, photographed at different events, with different women on his arm, none of them Ally.

The rest of the night he read in the rocking chair, then lay in bed listening to the rhythm of the crickets. Things would return to normal. Soon, she'd cross his mind less and less. He kept reminding himself of that throughout the night and into the next day, but as he stood in the middle of the bakery kitchen, all he could think about was Ally.

"We have four weddings this weekend, so we'll have to split up delivering goods to the events," Frank said, as he looked at the calendar. Ally's system for weddings was on a spreadsheet on the laptop, but Frank was still using his own system, written in a lined notebook.

Things didn't run as smoothly without her, but they ran well enough. There were little things she'd have thought to do, but between Frank and David on the phone, they got through the day. Michael had tried to think of a way to ask about Ally, but chickened out. Did she make it back safe? Was she glad to be back? Did she miss Camden Cove?

"Was Ally's flight okay?" It was neutral enough to start the conversation, he figured.

"Yes, on time and everything." Frank looked up from his notebook, tapping his pencil on the counter. "You know, I was surprised she didn't take our offer of the bakery."

"What do you mean?"

"She seemed happier baking here with you than in Paris."

"What?"

"I don't know, I just got a feeling." Frank shrugged. "Obviously I was wrong, but she always seems stressed out, over there."

"I can't believe she isn't running her own kitchen, with her talent." She had more skill than he'd ever seen in a chef. She certainly shouldn't be standing in the shadows. Her images should be connected to a famous patisserie.

"Don't I know it?" Frank sighed. "But I seem to be wrong about a lot of things."

Michael wanted to fish, dig deeper into Ally through Frank, but he let it go as Frank got distracted with other things. His head spun. As cheesy as it sounded, he wanted her to be all that she could be. It wasn't necessarily Jean-Paul holding her back, but Ally herself.

~

Ally stood in front of the mirror, holding another dress up in front of her. She swirled her torso as the red dress floated with her movements. It was strapless, and perfect for the summer night. An Italian design every woman looked beautiful in. She pulled it over her head and zipped up the side. She looked at herself, her eyes with deep purple bags beneath them. The dress didn't hide any of her feelings.

When Jean-Paul showed up, he wrapped his arms around her waist and kissed the back of her neck. She leaned into it just a bit, but she felt cold.

He kissed her again and said, "Don't forget a shawl. We should take a walk after."

"Oui."

She tried to shake off whatever she was feeling. Tonight was the kind of night she had dreamt about as a little girl. Le Basilic nestled in the Abbesses Quarter. For Paris, 1905 hardly made this building old, but something about it screamed *La Ville Lumière*. Maybe it was the vines climbing around the entrance, the heavy curtain flanking the doorway, or the dining room fireplace, but the restaurant always made her feel like she was in a Parisian film.

Jean-Paul held her hand most of the way. When they arrived, the night air had just cooled enough to wear her shawl. He'd been especially affectionate, which was throwing her off, because she was usually the one giving.

Inside, the room was illuminated by candlelight. The dark wood paneling reflected the golden glow. The waiter ushered them to a seat against the wall, and she slid into the booth. She let the night play out before her. Life was almost back to normal, at least on the outside. Jean-Paul talked through dinner about the patisserie, about their friends, and all that happened while she was away.

"I talked to Michalak, and he's opening up a patisserie in London."

"Oh, really?" She thought nothing of it.

"They offered me the head chef position."

Ally looked up from the slice of duck she had been moving around with her fork. She set the utensil down on the plate. "Are you going to take it?"

"Well, I'm not sure. I wanted to talk to you, of course." He cut another piece of meat as he chewed. "This could be big for my career."

Her heart pounded like a jackhammer inside her chest. He had been shopping around for a new job?

He sat up straight. "I tried to tell you, but you didn't call."

"You didn't want the calls. Remember?" She played with her napkin in her lap. Her chest felt hot. "You wanted to miss me."

He made shushing gestures. "Calm down, Ally."

"You were looking for another job?"

He shook his head. "They came to me."

He reached inside his jacket pocket and pulled out a velvet box. Her hands instantly covered her mouth. This was it. In her favorite restaurant, in the heart of Paris. People around them noticed what was going on and watched. Ally looked around, trying to take everything in, and then he took her hand. The box opened and her mouth fell open as she looked down at… a pin. The box, she realized, was a chintzy faux velvet. Inside was a lapel pin in the shape of a red London telephone box. "Come to London with me."

"It's a pin?" Ally's face heated, and perspiration prickled the back of her neck. She had given everything up for a *pin*? "Did you take the job?"

"Not yet." He closed the box with a snap and put it back into his pocket, then took both of her hands in his. "Come with me."

People still had their eyes on them, making embarrassment

heat up her neck and face. Her heart deflated as she sat there listening to Jean-Paul.

"London?" She shook her head. "I thought you'd never leave Paris? You said you hated London."

"I don't hate the money. I told him I wanted you to come, too. What do you think?"

"That I didn't even know about this until five minutes ago." Did he expect an instant answer?

"I thought we'd be celebrating, not fighting over this." He waved at a waiter. "Let's order champagne."

"I thought you wanted our own patisserie at some point?" Ally ran through all their conversations over the past two years. They'd rent a place, kitchen big enough for two chefs, a small coffee selection, a few hors d'oeuvres. "To run together."

"You could run your station, like here." He said it as though he had discovered the answer to their problems, but the problem was much more complicated. "This is how we get there. Stepping stones to the end goal."

"What about Paris?" She wasn't sure she understood what was happening. Jean-Paul faded off in the background as her head took over, repeating the word *London* and flashing the pin in her head.

Jean-Paul grabbed her hands again and brought them to his lips. "My love, we will always have Paris."

CHAPTER 14

*M*ichael had the mixer running when Frank came up and handed him a notebook.

"Is this Ally's?" he said.

Michael looked at the familiar notebook. The one she had written all her ideas for a cookbook inside. She'd left it behind?

"I bet she'd like that back," he said.

"I better ship this over to her," Frank said, grabbing a pen and a piece of paper. He wrote down the address from his contacts.

"Do you want me to run this to the post office?" Michael asked, not sure why he was volunteering.

"You don't mind?" Frank smiled. "I have the address right here."

He handed over the piece of paper with Ally's address written neatly on it.

Michael took a deep breath. "It's no problem. I can swing by on my way to see my mom."

"Great, Ally will really appreciate you sending it to her."

A day later, Michael looked at the envelope, then at a blank sheet of paper. Was he being totally weird, writing a letter? He grabbed a pen and wrote.

Ally,

Looks like you accidentally left this behind.

Hope all is well,

Michael

Simple. Nothing more needed to be said. He did what he had to do.

Done.

He looked at the paper, tapping the pen on his kitchen table.

He should've mailed it the night before, when Frank had asked him to do it. But he needed to write something. He had to write *something*.

P.S. I'm sorry for being a tool.

Now he was done.

He folded up the paper into the manila envelope with her notebook and put the stamps on the front. As he got up, the chair creaked underneath him, the way his bones sounded recently. He had been working from morning to night. Not that he minded, but he had missed seeing his mother for the past few days, and his yard had seen better times.

He stuffed the envelope into the mailbox, then stood there, staring at it.

He needed to write more.

No. He shook his head. He didn't. She had clearly made her choice. His eyes stayed on the word *Paris* written on the package. Down the road, he could see Peggy Miller, the mail carrier, doing her rounds. He didn't have much time if he was to write another letter, but what would he say? Would she even want to hear from him? He had been a total jerk.

Without thinking, he grabbed the package out of the mailbox and ran back inside the house. He swiped the pen off the table and looked for the books. The books he bought for her before she left. There they sat on the side table, right where he left it. He ripped open the envelope's seal and before he put the books in, he wrote on one the inside covers.

It's no La Femme Actuelle, *but you should probably read real French literature at some point.*

Michael

He stuffed Balzac's *The Black Sheep*, with Hemingway's *The Sun Also Rises,* written in Paris, into the envelope. From the junk drawer, he grabbed some packaging tape and ripped off a long piece with his teeth. He slapped the tape over the broken seal, jumped into his truck, and headed to the post office.

"Good morning, Michael," Peggy said as he reached the counter. She had been working at the post office since he was a kid.

"Peggy," he greeted her, handing over the package.

"Paris? Huh?" She looked at the address.

The whole town was nosy. "It's for Ally Williams, Frank and David's daughter. She needs a notebook sent back to her. She left it behind at the bakery."

She bounced the package in her hand. "It feels like more than a notebook."

"Isn't it illegal to go through people's mail?"

Peggy laughed like he was being ridiculous. "I'm not going through anybody's mail, just feeling it."

He nodded once and left. He didn't want to linger any longer, lest he change his mind.

Ally had thought coming back to Paris would bring more clarity to her life, but things just got more complicated. Jean-Paul had been on cloud nine about his new job. When they got home from the restaurant, she feigned a headache. After he left, she lay awake, thinking about following Jean-Paul. Wouldn't he move for her? This was a huge opportunity for Jean-Paul. Was she being selfish if she wasn't happy for him?

The next morning, at the bakery, Jean-Paul greeted her with kissing her neck and whispered French poetry.

"I'm going to see Lucius Michalak this afternoon, about

London," he said. "He said he wants the bakery opened as soon as they finish renovating it all."

Throughout the day, her head spun with all the changes happening around her. She took a walk at lunch, thinking of London. A new city, a new job, a new life. The cobblestone streets filled with tourists made her feel like a pinball, bouncing back and forth through mobs of tour groups.

When she returned to the patisserie after lunch, there was a buzz as everyone looked curiously at Jean-Paul's office. She glanced at Margot as she put her things in her locker. "What's going on?"

"Jean-Paul's been talking with Lucius for over an hour."

"Oh." Ally swung around and looked toward Jean-Paul's office.

Through the glass, she saw him standing behind his desk. Lucius Michalak sat in a chair, leaning back with one leg crossed over the other. Jean-Paul looked ecstatic. He flailed his arms out as they spoke, but nothing being said made it through the glass walls. They kissed each other's cheeks like true Parisians, and Michalak walked out past Ally, straight through the kitchen and out the door.

Ally headed to the office. "Was that about London?"

"He wants me to start right away."

"What do you mean, right away?" Her throat dried up. "When would you leave?"

"I'm leaving tonight." He stared out beyond her, his face beaming. "I'm leaving tonight on his private jet."

"Wow." It sounded as though he over-pronounced the word *I'm* to her. "We're leaving tonight?"

"Well, not exactly... you see, Michalak wants all my attention on getting everything ready for the opening." He walked around to the other side of his desk. "Setting up the décor, the menu, etc. I need to do some things on the business side, and I've been asked to be on a British baking show."

"Not *the* British Baking Show?" Her eyes widened. "That's amazing!"

"I think you should stay here until things settle down, and then come up."

"But when would that be?" She looked out the glass as the workers suddenly shuffled around the kitchen, pretending to be working and not listening to them.

Jean-Paul shrugged. "I don't own the restaurant, Ally. I can't just demand a sous chef. I can recommend one, but it's up to Lucius Michalak, really."

"But... you're the head chef, which means you're in charge of hiring." Ally couldn't believe what had just happened. "Unless I wasn't offered a position..."

He fumbled around with the papers on his desk. "Maybe I could recommend you for my position here."

"What?" Her heart sank.

"This is a great opportunity for me." Jean-Paul wasn't going to stay for her, or bring her with him.

"What about us?"

"Mon amour, there will always be us," he said, then again in French. "Il y aura toujours nous."

"But when will we ever see each other?" Ally wondered if this was what happened with the women before her. The end came and went before they knew what was happening.

"We can travel back and forth for a bit." Jean-Paul grabbed her hand and kissed it. "I wouldn't expect you to hold back for me."

Ally almost laughed, but covered her mouth. How could he say that? She had passed everything up for him.

She didn't hear the rest of what came out of his mouth. She just walked out of the office, slamming the door so hard she was sure the glass door would shatter behind her. Margot clapped as Ally marched by her and out the door.

She walked the street in a fog. She never wanted to go back to his apartment, but she had some of her stuff there. She wasn't sure if they had broken up officially, but she knew they were no longer together. She walked up the hill to the Basilica, the summer heat still radiating out of the pavement. Even when the darkness of night came, tourists still crowded the streets of the eighteenth arrondissement. She couldn't avoid people, and all she wanted was to be alone.

What would she tell her dads? She'd definitely get a big fat *told you so* from them.

Margot texted her throughout the night, begging her to go out with her. With nowhere else to go, Ally agreed to meet her friends.

"He's a connard!" Margot yelled over the crowd at the bar. She held onto her glass of merlot for dear life.

"I can't believe he didn't fight for me." Ally cried over her glass of white wine.

"He didn't even want me to come," Ally mumbled over her glass of red wine.

"All men are connards!" Margot yelled out again, and an old man tapped his glass against hers. "Especially French men."

"Not all guys are jerks." Ally thought of Michael and what a jerk she had been to *him*.

"Well, all men in this city only have one thing on their minds." Margot's voice carried further to a group of women twice their age. Her accent grew thicker the more wine they drank.

"It never changes!" a woman agreed with them from the next table. She lifted her glass to them.

Ally checked her phone. Jean-Paul would be gone by now, already on his way to London. She finished her drink, kissed Margot and her new friend Celine on the cheeks.

She took a taxi back to her apartment. She opened the front door to the lobby, fumbling with her keys. When she finally got in the elevator, she leaned against the rickety box, holding her head between her hands.

When the doors opened, she noticed the note.

Ally,

Mon Amour

You can stay at my place until my lease runs out.

Come visit me in London!

Nous aurons toujours Paris!

Jean-Paul

She tossed the note aside and opened the door, hitting a package on the edge of the table. She recognized the zip code in the top corner first. Camden Cove.

She looked at the return address. Michael Mailloux.

It felt heavy. She ripped the envelope open and looked inside. Books. She dug her hand in and pulled out her notebook with two other books.

"*The Black Sheep.*" She laughed. The most depressing book of all time. Then Ernest Hemingway's *The Sun Also Rises*.

She pulled out her phone and started texting, but stopped herself.

She ran to her room, grabbed a piece of paper and pen, and started writing.

CHAPTER 15

$\mathcal{M}$ichael started bringing treats when he visited his mother. He had almost forgotten he had really learned how to bake from her. Before things got bad between his parents, she'd bake all kinds of desserts. Cakes, cookies, brownies, all her own recipes. She had been good at baking sweets, and his dad would always compliment her on them.

His dad would probably give him a hard time if he knew he'd turned into a pastry chef. He could almost hear the insults he'd sling if he knew. Not that he'd ever find out. He hadn't spoken to his father since before he left for the Marines.

When he came back from Afghanistan, he thought things would be better. The nightmares not so bad, and the day terrors dwindling. The VA gave as much help as they could, and Michael had been lucky. He had been open to interventions like therapy and different types of support systems. But other guys weren't so willing or lucky to have the help that he did.

As he walked through the sliding doors to his mother's wing, his body started to tense up and the usual assortment of feelings leaked in. Would it be a "repeat" day, or would she cry the whole time? Would she remember who he was, or had she stopped doing that?

How much had changed from yesterday, and what would tomorrow look like?

"Hey, Ma." He said it without really saying it *to* her. He fell into the chair next to her, adjusting the blanket around her feet. "You look pretty today."

She looked over at him. Her hair had been curled under. "Do I know you?"

Michael didn't respond. He looked out the window to the trees beyond and thought about the ocean. She didn't ask any more questions that afternoon, as if following his lead.

When he pulled into his driveway, he almost skipped checking the mail, but changed his mind and walked down to the box. Pulling the lid down, he saw a large envelope stuffed tightly with a return address of Paris. He ripped the package open right there in the side of the street. Three books stacked together, and light blue letter in front.

He carefully stuck his finger under the flap and opened it, careful not to damage the contents. He pulled out the folded paper with Ally's handwriting.

Dear Michael,

Have my fathers driven you crazy yet?

Thank you for the most depressing titles of all time. You sent me Ernest Hemingway? Really? An American who lived in Paris? Come on, Mailloux. I expected more from you. I sent you some must-reads of your own, however, I'm afraid the uplifting personal stories in the introductions will ruin your melancholy demeanor.

I'm dying to hear about Harry and Eve. Did they end up having dinner at The Fish Market? Have they gone out again?

Did Sully's wife have the baby?

I haven't told anyone back home, but I'm starting my own baking classes.

I hope you're enjoying yourself at the bakery.

Ally

When he got inside, he set the letter on the table and pulled out the three books. *Pastries* by Peirre Hermè, *The Escoffier Cook-*

book and Guide to Fine Cooking, and Julia Child's *The Art of French Cooking.*

He couldn't stop smiling all night, even as he read through Julia's introduction.

Ally checked her reflection one last time in the mirror before answering the door. She had worn her cutest dress and apron. The drinks and snacks had been arranged on the table. The packets of recipes printed out. She had six English expats signed up for her first baking class in Jean-Paul's apartment.

The couple from the States arrived first.

"We lived outside of Los Angeles," the wife, Karen, explained as Ally offered them a drink and some pastries. "I saw your class, and I thought… why not?"

The doorbell rang again and a woman, maybe in her eighties, stood at the door with a man standing behind her. The man spoke broken English. "This is Dorothy. She is here to take class?"

"Yes, Dorothy, please come in." Ally eyed the tall and handsome young escort.

He guided Dorothy in slowly as she used her cane to walk. She wore a nice dress and jewelry, her hair pulled back into a French twist. Pearls draped her neck.

"Alphonse would have just loved learning how to bake his favorite, *au bon pain,*" Dorothy said to the man as she settled into her seat at the counter.

The couple started talking to Dorothy about being transferred from the States, and she told them about when she moved from Dorset County in England in 1954. "Alphonse and I had four children here."

The couple's eyes warmed. "We hope to have children soon."

The man left Dorothy and told Ally he'd be back to pick her up. "She's all set, then?"

"She's old, not stupid," he said, his back to her as he headed down the hallway.

"Goodbye, darling," Dorothy said, and turned to the couple. "Samir is the best neighbor I've ever had."

As Samir stepped on the elevator, Ally called out, "I don't have your number!"

What if there was an emergency?

A middle-aged man exited the elevator, passing Samir.

"You must be Mr. Peters." He removed his hat and reached out to shake her hand.

"Yes." He didn't look at her, but at his shoes.

"Come in, I have a spot by Dorothy."

He followed Ally into the kitchen. He sat down in the empty chair next to Dorothy, his eyes glued to the countertop.

"Where do you come from, young man?" Dorothy asked.

Mr. Peters looked up, pushing his glasses into place. "All over, really. I move every few years, for work."

Dorothy smiled with curiosity as an awkward silence filled the room, just as the doorbell rang again and Ally ran to answer the door.

"Hello!" she said, swinging the door open.

"Good day!" Two men stood there in flip flops. They had to be Todd and Miles, the Australian men whose perfect bleached blond hair was like something you'd see in magazines.

Models.

"Come in!" She giggled to herself at the two's summer attire of pastel colors over their perfectly tanned skin. They sat down next to the couple from the States.

Ally offered everyone a drink and a plate of pastries, outputting off the inevitable. She wished Michael was there with her. Then, without thinking about it anymore, she stepped in front of the kitchen island and started her first Parisian pastry lesson.

"Welcome. I'm absolutely delighted to have you all here tonight." She folded her hands in front of her so she wouldn't play with them as she spoke. "My name is Ally Williams, and I grew up in Maine, in the States." She paused and grabbed her glass of water, taking a sip. Her mouth was dry. "Baking is in my blood. My father is a master pastry chef who studied and trained in Paris. After high school, I followed in his footsteps, moving from Maine to Montreal, then overseas to Paris, working at La Patisserie Michalak, here in the city. My passion is French baking, but my other passion is teaching my tricks and tips to others, to help them master the French pastry. Each week, I will run a baking class with classics like the macaron, the éclair, or the sweet mille-fuielle. Tonight, however, we're going bake the classic *pain au chocolat*."

She had all the ingredients set out in front of each person, just like the night with Michael. As she went through each step, the class followed along. The couple from the states, Jamie and Karen, pulled out two bottles of wine from their bag and shared a glass with everyone.

Ally had them drop the yeast in the warm water first. "We're going to make the dough, but you need to refrigerate it for two hours before working with it, so I've prepared dough for you to work with while your dough is cooling." Once the dough was in the refrigerator and the pre-made dough in front of each student, Ally said, "Now, you're going to pound the butter into a six-inch wide, half-inch thick square. I use cellophane to help with rolling."

She grabbed her homemade butter and rolled it out in between two pieces of cellophane. When she finished, she slapped the top and wiped her hands on a dishtowel. She walked around the room, watching as the others pounded out their butter.

"Do you always make your own butter?" Miles asked.

Ally loved answering the questions. Her experience showed through in her answers. "No, of course not, but in my patisserie, I use only the finest ingredients, because I'm making the finest of foods. Baking also becomes easier with fresh, simple ingredients."

"I'd imagine it's more malleable for folding into the flour, being less processed," Karen said.

"French cooking in general is more about the freshest, best-quality ingredients," Dorothy spoke up from her table with Mr. Peters.

"It's certainly not about convenience." Ally laughed at how long she had prepped for this class tonight. "Okay, those squares look great. Set those aside for a moment and take out your dough."

Each student grabbed a flat block of perfect dough.

"The first thing we're going to do is sprinkle a little bit of flour on the dough and our work surface." Ally pulled off the cellophane and dusted the top, rubbing the cool surface with her hand. "We want our butter to be two-thirds the size of our dough." She began to roll it out with her rolling pin, exaggerating her motions. "Make sure your edges are nice and square all of the time."

When she finished, she walked around the room, helping each one of them as they rolled. When everyone's dough looked good, she modeled how to use the small offset spatula to place the butter on the dough. Then she began the folding process.

"Don't forget to brush off that excess flour, we don't want that in the pastry." She examined their efforts as they brushed away the extra flour and folded.

"It looks like a little pillow," Dorothy said to Mr. Peters, who nodded his head as he pulled the dough to fit each edge.

"That's a perfect seal," Ally said to Jamie, who looked unsure. He held his rolling pin with white knuckles. "Now, roll it out."

"Are you sure I'm not messing this up?" he asked, as he pushed the rolling pin over the hump of dough.

"You're doing fine," Ally laughed, walking to the next table. "You're all doing great!" She paused for a moment. "Okay, now you've done one turn, but the dough will need four turns, with refrigeration time in between each turn. Since we can't stay all night, I have more premade dough that's ready to go."

"You've thought of everything," Todd said.

Everyone agreed.

The rest of the night went better than she could have ever expected. The couples and the models, who turned out to be roommates, got along brilliantly and even signed up for the next class before heading out for drinks together. Samir showed up ten minutes before the end of class to pick up Dorothy, but waited around for another half hour as Dorothy discussed up-and-coming artists with Mr. Peters and Ally. Everyone left with a pink pastry box of pains au chocolat, even Samir.

She looked around the kitchen, her whole body buzzing. Her gut reaction was to call Michael and tell him how it went, but when the sudden realization that her life was in shambles washed over her, she shoved her phone back in her pocket. This big, beautiful kitchen was not hers, but Jean-Paul's, and for less than a month. Where would she get the kitchen space to continue her cooking classes? Her salary as an assistant chef certainly wouldn't allow for it. Jean-Paul could barely afford this place.

One class wasn't going to change those facts.

She put the phone down. She couldn't call her dads, or Mom and Martin. She wouldn't be able to lie much longer about everything, but tonight she didn't want to ruin how she felt.

The glaring option she did have, would be to go back home, but she couldn't do that to Michael. This was his only chance to have a kitchen. She couldn't take that away from him.

Michael cleaned the counters as Frank calculated the receipts from the special orders at the desk in the kitchen.

"We have so many weddings coming up, I'm not sure we can do it all." Frank pulled off his glasses and rubbed between his eyes.

Michael had learned that Frank tended to be overly dramatic when it came to pretty much everything, and not to be too concerned by his worry. Although, he had thought the same thing once the summer waned into fall.

"I didn't realize weddings were so popular this time of year."

"When we partnered up with the local bed and breakfasts and inns in town, it pulled in a lot of business for us." Frank's cheeks puffed out. "I guess that's a problem I can live with, for now."

Michael threw a dish towel over his shoulder and pulled out the croissant dough to turn one last time.

"Have you talked to Ally?" Frank asked.

Michael rolled out the dough. "Nope, not since the package."

Frank tapped his foot with more and more vigor the longer he sat there. Michael tried to ignore the intense bobbing as he worked the dough, but he had known Frank long enough that he had something on his mind.

"Is there something bothering you, Frank?"

He turned. "I wasn't going to say anything, but since you've asked..."

Michael wished he hadn't asked.

"David told me that I shouldn't meddle, but I just can't sit back and watch her throw her life away for a guy who doesn't care about her!" Frank's voice rose from a quiet murmur to a full battle cry.

Michael continued to roll the dough out from the middle to the edges, trying not to engage. Frank pointed at him. "You understand her."

Michael shook his head. He picked up the rolling pin and began working on the dough again. "It's not going to happen, Frank."

"Why?" Frank asked. "Don't you see it?"

Michael didn't allow himself to feel anymore, otherwise he'd never be able to handle what he had been through and seen in his life. Why was it any different with Ally?

"It doesn't matter what I think. She made it very clear to me that she was not interested."

"Ah, but that, right there, is the problem. You see, I don't think she knows how she feels when she's here."

Michael pulled out a piece of cellophane and wrapped the block of dough, ready for tomorrow. He wanted Frank to stop, so he can bury his feelings as deep as possible. "Listen Frank, I think your husband's right."

Frank looked confused. "David's right? About what?"

"You shouldn't meddle."

Michael opened the fridge, placed the dough inside, did one last check to make sure everything was prepped, and gave Frank a salute. He still seemed confused as Michael headed out the back door. He threw his helmet on, snapping on the chin strap and turning on his bike's engine. He sat staring out at the water. Little signs of fall were creeping in, and the crowds dwindled at the beach. Ally's summer visit was now just a memory.

He didn't head home like he usually would after work. Instead, he drove up Route 1A along the coast to clear his head. But all it did was give him more freedom to think, and he was done with thinking. By the time he showed up for poker night, his head was in such disarray he almost wished he had skipped it altogether.

Harry stood washing dishes as Michael walked in. He threw his helmet on the bench beside the door.

"Where's everyone?" he asked, looking around the empty living room. "No dip, again?"

Harry wiped his hands with a towel. "Hey, haven't you checked your text messages?"

Michael pulled out his phone. "No, what?"

Then he hit his home button. Messages filled the screen.

"Sully's wife is having the baby."

"Oh."

Sully had been Michael's closest friend since he was a kid. Why wasn't he happy for him?

"Want to stay and watch the game with me?" Harry had the television tuned to the Sox game.

"No, I think I'll just head home." Michael grabbed his helmet, worried about going home to an empty house, but not in the right headspace to sit with Harry and watch baseball.

"Suit yourself." Harry walked to the couch. "I do have dip in the fridge."

Michael blinked as Harry's motions suddenly seemed to slow down. His vision became a bit tunneled and the room swayed, even though he knew he wasn't moving. Fuzzy black shadows lurked in his peripheral vision. He had been through this enough times to recognize the symptoms.

He should stay.

He strapped his helmet on. "Nah, man, I'll just go."

He climbed down the porch steps, feeling the heat rash running up his neck. Being alone would be worse for him. His triggers were always heightened in his empty house. His anxiety pulsed, frantic. His heart pounding inside his chest. This was the second attack this week. Things weren't getting better, like he'd thought they were… while Ally was around.

When he pulled into his mother's driveway, he stayed on the porch until his breath returned to normal. The rest of the night he baked in his kitchen, pounding out cake after cake. He should just call her. He should call Harry, or his sponsor. He thought about the letter, and how Ally told him about starting her own cooking classes. Frank might be right. The guy wasn't right for her.

But as he looked around his kitchen, cakes everywhere, his mania made visible in pastries, neither was he.

CHAPTER 16

$\mathcal{A}$lly kept showing up to work at La Patisserie Michalak, even though each day she was sure the new chef would fire her. He kept his eye on her through the glass-windowed office as she made her pastries.

Just as memories of the summer started playing in her head, the new head chef headed toward her station and watched her for more than a minute before speaking.

"You're very good," he said in broken English, as though he was surprised. "Jean-Paul didn't tell me you were this good."

The sting made her slap the dough. "Non, je suis sûr qu'il ne me le dit pas."

He looked her over again. Her French had never been very good, but she couldn't tell if Chef Remi kept nodding his head as though he was agreeing with her or something else inside his head before he left. She returned to her tarte, forming the dough around the individual baking pan.

After work, she walked home, planning out her next class. She would have her students make apple turnovers with fresh fall apples. They would have two hours, which would give plenty of time even to make the dough.

Stepping into the lobby, she stopped at the mailboxes before going up. She leafed through her junk mail, mostly credit cards and surveys, but crammed in the back sat another package from Camden Cove.

Michael.

She tore it open right there in the lobby. Inside, she found two more books, a leather journal and a handwritten note.

Ernest Hemingway lived at 74 rue Cardinal Lemione, and wrote some of his greatest works there, including The Sun Also Rises. *The Moveable Table, his memoir of living in Paris, was another.*

Hopefully the following will be up to your Highness' standards.

Harry and Eve have gone out on two more "official" dates, but don't ask any more. I've been out of middle school for years.

Sully had a boy named Oliver Michael.

How did your cooking class go? You should think about your craquelines.

Michael

P.S. Here's a real journal for your recipes.

She stared at the journal with her name engraved into the leather.

Then she slid the rest of the books out of the envelope. One was an English translation of *The Book of the City of Ladies* by Christine de Pizan, and Marcel Proust's *In Search of Lost Time.* She leafed through each book, looking for more clues to Michael within the pages.

She wished he had written more questions in his letter.

That night, she needed to prep for her cooking class, but before she did, she wrote Michael back. She ran the letter out to the post as soon as she finished. The rest of the night, she hummed to the radio as she prepped for class, getting everything ready for her students. When she climbed into bed, she pulled out Proust. A bit heavy for bedtime, but Proust was a surprise. She liked his writing. She fell asleep as the storyteller dipped a madeleine into his tea at Combray.

~

Michael helped set up the folding chairs in a circle. Pastor Meryle always ran the AA meetings on Sunday nights. "To start off the week with the right mindset," he'd tell the group. Tonight, however, was a special meeting. The group had promised to meet Michael tonight, even though it was a Tuesday.

"How's your mother?" the pastor asked, filling the coffee filter with the aromatic grounds of Folgers.

"The same."

Pastor Meryle patted him on the back. "She'd be really proud of you tonight."

Michael had started going to the meetings years back, a little bit after his mom left the house. It had been his lowest point. He had been working at the Fish Market, kept a job well enough, but the quiet solitude of his mother's house drove him mad. He'd drink until he passed out, and start all over again the next day.

Tonight, however, was Michael's fifth year sober. Eighth year since the roadside bomb and Peter's death. Twelfth year since he said good-bye to his mom before she became sick. Twenty-Five since his dad left.

Some of the regulars came, mostly the old timers, but Harry showed up with Sully.

"What's it like being a dad?" Michael felt bad that he hadn't visited since the hospital.

"I don't sleep anymore. But he's cute like a leprechaun."

"You're calling your own kid a leprechaun?" Harry shook his head. "That's horrible."

"He'd better be Irish-looking, with a name like Oliver O'Sullivan." Sully hit Michael in the arm, laughing at Harry.

"Gentlemen, why don't we all take a seat, so we can get to the cookies," Pastor Meryle said, gesturing toward the folding chairs.

Sully and Harry moved to the seats.

"As all of you know, tonight marks Michael's fifth year sober!" the pastor announced to the group of a dozen or so people. Everyone clapped. "We wanted to mark this day by having a celebration of Michael's strength and perseverance, but also come together to support each other in reaching goals like this. So, as tradition, when we reach this milestone, we ask that people tell their story if they can, and Michael has agreed."

Everyone clapped as Michael stood up. He hadn't spoken since the first meeting, when he introduced himself. "Hi, my name is Michael, and I'm an alcoholic."

"Hi, Michael."

"Today is my fifth year sober." The group, well mainly Sully, clapped again. Michael rubbed his sweaty palms on his pants and continued. "Five years ago, I sat at my kitchen table with an empty bottle of whiskey in one hand and a Smith and Wesson in the other. The only reason I'm alive today is because Pastor Meryle happened to stop by my house that night to check in on me. Talk about divine intervention." The crowd chuckled in a sad way. They, too, understood what it was like to hit rock bottom. "Drinking had been my way to escape the nightmares, and the pain of reality. Drinking was my way to move through it, to cover up how I really felt. My friends had no idea, my mother was too sick to notice, and I gave everyone else the Michael they wanted to see, because it was easier than showing the real one.

"By the time Pastor Meryle stopped by, I had never felt more alone in my life." He took in a breath, holding it in for a moment before releasing it. "But that's the thing about alcohol. It makes you feel like it's the only thing there for you. Booze didn't want me to see that I wasn't alone. I had friends. Great friends. I had my job. I also had my community." He looked out at the familiar faces. "I wasn't alone, and neither are any of you. I couldn't have gotten through five years without all of you in my life. So, I want to thank you for helping me get here."

Mary, one of the old timers, hurried over to Michael, giving him a hug when he finished. "I'm so proud of you."

Harry and Sully came to him next, patting him on the back. As he held the black medallion in his hand, he wondered if anyone saw through his act. If they saw how very, truly, alone he still felt.

"I better get going." Sully dumped his empty coffee cup into the trash.

Michael nodded. "Give my love to the wife and kid."

"Can you believe I'm a dad?"

"No," Michael said, as Sully play-punched him in the stomach. "We still can't believe Krissy married you."

"Ha, ha," Sully said. "See you losers later." Sully shook Pastor Meryle's hand as he left.

"You want to grab a bite to eat?" Harry asked.

Michael didn't. He wanted to go home and be alone, but Harry had come to support him. He looked at the time, already past seven. "Where?"

"I was thinking the tavern?"

He nodded. "Sure."

"Meet me there?"

"It's a date."

"Or is that weird, going to a bar on your sobriety anniversary?"

"Do we have another option at this time?"

"No."

"Wherever is fine." Michael's voice came out short. He said goodbye to the others and met Harry in the parking lot.

"So, I'll meet you there?" Harry asked as he reached his sedan.

"Yup." Michael let out a huff.

Harry stopped in the middle of the parking lot and faced him. "It's none of my business, but ever since Ally left, you've been more like the old Michael."

Michael froze, his body rigid. "What's that supposed to mean?"

"It means I'm worried about you." Harry looked around before saying. "You've been holed up in your house, or the bakery."

"I've just started a new job, give a man a break."

"Is it just this new job, or is it her?"

"She has nothing to do with it."

Harry rubbed his face. "Michael, I know you. She has every-thing to do with it."

"Just because you've got your own thing going on, doesn't mean everyone needs to be in a relationship."

"She told me that she and Jean-Paul broke up."

"What? They broke up?"

"You should call her."

Michael backed away. "I think I am going to skip dinner. Tired, you know."

He ignored Harry as he yelled out to him. He didn't even hear what he had to say, the noise in his mind too loud.

He wanted to go home, be by himself, but when he got there, he didn't get out of his truck, just stared out at the dark, empty house. From the corner of his eye, he saw the post box. Was he a glutton for punishment? Jumping out of the truck, his stomach sank as he opened the mailbox and at first saw nothing. But then in the back, he saw one blue envelope from Paris.

He opened it immediately.

Dear Michael,

My class went better than I could've hoped for, being alone this time. I had six students and I did the exact same class with the pains au chocolat. I even weighed everything out beforehand and made the doughs. It all went smoothly. The students were this eclectic group of expats and they all signed up for another class tomorrow night. We're making chaussons. *Apple season has begun over here.*

How's the bakery? Are you enjoying it? Are they allowing you to make decisions about the menu?

I hope they recognize your talent!

How's Oliver? And Sully and his wife? Has Harry taken Eve letter-boxing? Have you changed anything on the menu?

I've included some light reading.

Ally

P.S. When it comes to the menu, if you can get Frank on your side, David will almost always cave.

P.P.S. I'm moving. Below is my new address.

He read it twice before going inside. There wasn't a lot said, but what wasn't said was huge. She didn't mention Jean-Paul.

At all.

~

The whole morning Ally looked for a new apartment, one where she could hold a few people in a kitchen for small cooking classes. But the options looked too sketchy or too pricey. When her search ran dry, she sat in her rented room, on her bed, typing more recipes out. She had photographed as much of her pastries as she could the other night at Jean-Paul's. His kitchen screamed Paris, with his copper pots hanging from a brass rack. She had been on edge all day about the class, so when Remy, her roommate, told her about her recent engagement, she didn't pick up on the fact Remy was asking her to leave.

"Oh," Ally blinked at the clock. Less than an hour, she had class. "When do you need me out?"

Remy frowned in a sympathetic way. "As soon as you can find a place."

Her stomach twisted in worry by the vagueness of her answer. Did that mean now?

As she stepped into Jean-Paul's empty apartment, ending the one thing that kept her going, she had never felt so low.

Once everyone showed up, her nerves calmed. Mr. Peters and Dorothy showed up first, with Samir.

"Would you like to stay, Samir?" Ally could push Dorothy and Mr. Peters closer together at their table.

Samir shook his head. "No, merci. Next time."

"Well, I'm not sure there will be a next time." Ally decided it was unrealistic to continue to pretend, even for tonight. "This is it, it looks like."

Dorothy opened her mouth. "Oh, dear. I've quite looked forward to this weekly engagement."

"I know, I'm sorry." Ally may have been better off not starting

160

the classes after all. Would she upset more than just Dorothy? "This isn't my place and the owner is moving. I thought I'd find something bigger, but I'm afraid not."

"That's such a shame." Dorothy sat as Samir pushed her stool in.

"Yes, such a shame," Mr. Peters agreed, sitting next to Dorothy.

"I just rented out a small studio a few blocks away. " Dorothy pointed at her. "Let me ask around."

The rest of the class showed up at the same time, both with bottles of wine in hand. Miles poured glasses for everyone as they all reacquainted themselves. Samir stayed for a drink, but left Dorothy with the others and promised to pick her and Mr. Peters up at the end.

"Welcome back everyone, tonight we're going to be baking with these delicious apples." She had placed wicker baskets with freshly picked apples on each table. "We're going to bake *chausson aux pommes,* or apple turnovers."

The night went just as smoothly as the last. Ally became comfortable in front of them as she shared her love of baking. Teaching had been such a pleasant surprise to her. She loved the interaction and the excitement. She loved watching them create something incredible with their own hands.

"What's the next class?" Miles asked as he stirred his simmering apples.

Ally clasped her hands together and said, "I'm actually going to have to hold off classes for a while. I'm sorry."

"What do you mean?" Todd asked.

"Non." Ally shrugged. What else could she say?

"You could use my apartment," Dorothy said. "I have a fabulous kitchen that only Samir uses. It would be such a shame to not continue."

"Yes, you have to continue!" Karen said. "You could use our apartment, too."

"We can barely fit in our apartment, otherwise, we'd offer you a place," Miles said. He tasted his spoon, covered in sugary syrup, and moaned. "I want to learn more."

"But I'll have to bring a ton of ingredients and equipment."

"Nonsense." Dorothy waved her hand at Ally. "I will have Samir pick everything up for you. I'll stock the kitchen with what you need. And I have all the cookware you'd want in a French patisserie."

"But I'd have to prepare."

"You're welcome to come over any time if you need to prepare for class."

"I couldn't ask you to do all of that for me."

"Darling, we want you to continue to share your knowledge with us."

Ally hadn't thought of what she was doing as sharing, but as she looked out at the rest of the class, she wanted nothing more than to continue to share with these people. She just wished she could share with one more person, but he was too far away.

CHAPTER 17

*S*amir pulled up outside in a black Mercedes sedan with Dorothy in the back. Dorothy had offered to help Ally lug everything to her new apartment when Ally mentioned it would take a few trips on the Metro to move.

Ally had only a few boxes, her life's possessions didn't amount to much. As she looked back into her room before dropping her set of keys on the kitchen counter, it didn't look like she had ever been there.

She dumped a box in the trunk.

"Samir will help with your boxes and put everything in the boot," Dorothy said.

It only took Samir one trip to grab the rest of the boxes. He loaded them into the back and removed the last small box from Ally's hands. "Allow me."

"Merci."

He nodded, then opened the door for her with his free hand.

Ally leaned across the seat to kiss Dorothy on the cheeks. "I can't even begin to thank you."

"It was our pleasure."

The car dipped when Samir sat behind the wheel. Soon, they

traveled down the streets toward Ally's new apartment. She watched the basilica's dome fading away in the background.

"Thank you for doing this for me." Ally felt a bit embarrassed at having to reveal her circumstances. She was even more embarrassed about the things she hadn't told. Like how she gave up her fathers' bakery for a guy who never loved her.

"What's the next class going to be about?" Dorothy asked.

"I was thinking about doing crème brúlée." Ally thought about it and then changed her mind. "Maybe *palmiers*."

"Either would be an excellent choice." Dorothy patted Ally's hand.

"My friend Michael says I should do my *craquelines*, but I think I'll wait until some of the basics are mastered."

"Ah, there's that name again," Dorothy said.

"What?"

"Well, you've mentioned the name Michael a few times. I thought he was your boyfriend."

"Oh, no. Just a friend back home."

"You like him."

"Non." Ally shook her head. "He's just a friend."

Samir chimed in in his thick accent, looking in the rearview mirror. "Your eyes give you away."

Ally thought back to their kiss at Elizabeth's wedding. Her heart stopped as though electricity shot through it. Then she thought about his face when she came to the nursing home. How angry he was with her. She had blown it with Michael. He was being a nice guy, replying to her letters. Nothing more.

When they pulled up to her new building, Samir popped the trunk and they all went up the three flights of stairs and into her new place. The studio apartment was small, even by Paris standards. But it had a window looking out at the shared garden, a bit of counter space, and a clean bathroom.

"My kitchen will be better for classes," Dorothy said, looking around the tiny kitchen. She shook her head, looking out at the garden below. "Samir will pick you up and bring you home again. A single woman like you should be careful in this neighborhood."

Ally hadn't thought about her safety, but now she noticed the extra locks on the door. "Thanks, that would be great."

Dorothy and Samir kissed Ally on the cheek as they said goodbye, insisting Samir come back the next day with some furniture that Dorothy didn't need anymore. Once they left and Ally was alone, the studio apartment felt bare and empty.

Then, as if someone had heard her silent wish, there was a knock on the door. She peeked out of the peephole and saw Margot standing there with a bottle of wine.

"What are you doing here?" Ally asked as she swung the door open, relieved to see her friend, hugging her.

"I came to see your new place." Margot stepped in the door and stopped, looking around. "Oh, mon dieu."

"Is it that bad?" Ally suddenly saw the cracks in the wall and the broken light fixture on the ceiling.

"Non." But Margot couldn't hide her disapproval. "It's something."

Ally wished she could fall into a chair, sink down and wallow in her misery, but she didn't have a chair. The familiar lump stuck in her throat.

"Let's go shopping." Margot put the wine on the floor and grabbed Ally's hand. "We can make this place look great."

Ally wiped away a tear. "Do you think we can?"

"Yes, it's your new start, your new chapter as they say." Margot gestured toward the few boxes sitting in the middle of the room. "It's time to make Paris your home."

Home. The word played over and over in her mind. She had been chasing the idea since the day she left Paris as a little girl, yet, now, as she looked around the bare apartment in the City of Light, this was no more her home than Camden Cove or Montreal or anywhere else she lived. She only felt most at home when she was in a kitchen with Michael.

What had she done?

The bakery lit up, the light reflecting off the stainless-steel surfaces when Michael turned on the lights. He hung his bag on a hook and pulled out the notebook he had started with Ally. Almost all of the pages were filled with some sort of information about baking. For instance, Michael hadn't understood how important it was to organize the workspace with all the tools and ingredients ready before he started any recipe. Most of the dough he made could be temperamental, and if he didn't have the right utensil at the right temperature at the right time, his dough could lose structure. If over mixed, a sponge cake could become stiff and crumbly, not light and airy, which was what they were known for.

Luckily, most of his big mistakes had been sorted out by the time David came back to the bakery to run the business side of things, because David watched him like a hawk. He insisted it was to help, but Michael could see the heart condition wasn't slowing David down. He wondered if he regretted his rash decision to give Michael the chef position.

Michael could see where Ally got her natural teaching ability. David would check out what he was doing and interject his tips and tricks. Like how he shredded frozen butter into the dough.

"A lot of people try cutting it up into tiny pieces, but this works so much better." He grabbed a couple of ice cubes and held them in his hands. "But you have to keep your hands cold to get that crispy, flaky texture."

Michael enjoyed David's tricks, and he learned a lot, but having someone looking over his shoulder wasn't exactly what he had in mind when Frank and David offered him the position. So, Michael started coming to the bakery earlier to avoid David's vigilant eye, but that morning, David came early as well.

"I'm trying to schedule the rest of the cooking classes before the season ends." David opened his computer and sat at a stool at the island, watching as Michael sliced apples. Then, like always, he pointed out what Michael was doing wrong. "You don't want to cut all the way down."

Michael looked at his knife as it perfectly sliced a one-eighth inch of apple. "I don't?" He sighed, looking at the clock. He still had at least eight more hours.

"It's easier to cut if you keep it attached, then go back after its all cut."

Michael carried on, leaving the slice attached at the bottom of the apple. All of David's tips were smart baking practices that Michael still needed to figure out, but it was wearing on him. Frank had been the one who redirected David away from Michael, but it seemed as though David really didn't want to let go.

"You know, Jack would probably hire me back at The Fish Market," Michael said, separating the slices.

"What do you mean?" David asked. "When will you have time?"

"David, if you want to bake again, I can go back to The Fish Market."

David just stared at him. "Frank would kill me." He slouched in the stool. "It's just what I've done for my whole life."

Michael understood where the man was coming from. It was never easy to let go of something, especially when it was still right there in front of you. It was like that with his mom. He never let go of the hope that she'd be back to her old self each time he visited, setting himself up for disappointment every time.

"I should get out of your way." David stood and grabbed his computer. "I'll just work in the front."

Michael sighed. He didn't have time for dramatics, either. "No, don't do that. If I'm doing stuff wrong, I should fix it. It's your bakery."

David rested the computer on the counter. "I have complete faith in you, Michael. I am glad I trusted Ally's judgment and hired you. You're very talented, especially at running a kitchen. It's just that I don't seem to have much use here, anymore."

Michael hadn't thought about what it might be like for David, who probably had no intention of slowing down before the heart attack.

"I really can ask for my job back."

David shook his head. "No, we need you here."

Michael paused, trying to think of a way to politely ask him to sort of back off, but couldn't seem to find the right words, so he went back to the tarte.

Just as he was about to lay out the slices, David said, "You should start in the middle."

Ally stood in the middle of her apartment, holding a vase she had bought in Provence. It was all wrong. She'd have to move the desk to the other side of the room, and the day bed into the corner. Placing the vase on the windowsill, she pushed the bed along the wall to the other side of the room. Grunting, she added lamps to her mental list of needs for her new place. The single bulb chandelier made all the shadows come alive.

Just as she'd promised, Dorothy had sent Samir with a van full of antique furniture she swore was just sitting in storage.

"I have no use for them"

"What about your family? Wouldn't they want this stuff?"

Dorothy made a face. "My son doesn't want any of it. It's better if it goes to someone who needs it."

Ally looked at the pieces. She was almost positive the day bed was brand new.

She dragged the mahogany table to the other side of the room, stopping every few feet to see if she was making even more scratches in the parquet floors, but there were so many from the previous occupants, she couldn't tell.

"There," she said, putting her hands on her hips. The space was small. There was barely enough room for the few pieces she had. Definitely not big enough for two, like the advertisement said. The bathroom was clean, the kitchen had a foot of counter space, which in Paris, was a plus. The view was decent, the location not the greatest, but not the worst. As she circled the space, she decided that all in all, she'd done okay.

A tiny seed of pride grew in her chest. This was her place. She could do whatever, decorate however, and invite over whomever she wanted. She bounced on the bed, leaning back on her hands, smiling at the room. This was hers. All hers.

She wanted to do more classes.

She wanted to run more than one class a week. She wanted to have classes for all different levels of Parisian baking. She enjoyed her small group of students. After the past few sessions, the small group had become friends who enjoyed their time together. She had even been invited for dinner at Miles and Todd's. But she wanted to see what else she could do.

She had been working on her cookbook, using photographs of her work at Jean-Paul's or at the patisserie, afraid her tiny apartment wouldn't be a good backdrop. It would do, but a real kitchen was what she really wanted.

She wanted her own bakery.

CHAPTER 18

*I*t was no use. Paris didn't want a bakery like Ally envisioned. All the properties that were suitable for a patisserie were too small to operate, or too big to manage. What she really wanted was to bring the bakery in Camden Cove to Paris, which might be easier than finding an affordable place.

Ally scrolled the listings on her phone during her break. La Michalak had carried on without Jean-Paul, but was no longer the same. The new head chef was even more particular about pumping out quantity versus quality.

"Faire plus!" He'd yell out in the kitchen. "Do more!"

It had been weeks since she had spoken to Jean-Paul, and it seemed even longer since she received a letter in the mail from Michael. He hadn't written to her since she moved to her new place. Though, she hadn't written to him either. But she was the one who wrote last, she argued with herself, every time she thought about his lack of response. But she knew if she wanted to talk to him so bad, she should just text him. Tell him how she felt.

That she'd made a mistake that night in Camden Cove.

Looking back now, seeing how things ended up, she wasn't quite sure why she stopped him from kissing her. She had wanted to kiss him all night.

Yes, she had Jean-Paul, but that wasn't what stopped her. It was Paris. She couldn't ask Michael to leave everything behind, his career, his mother, his friends, all so that she could be in Paris.

Harry's warning made it obvious. Michael didn't need a woman like her. He had sacrificed too much for someone as selfish as her.

Her phone rang.

Adam was calling her.

The baby!

"Hello?"

"It's time!" Elizabeth screamed into the phone. "The baby's coming!"

Ally's heart dropped. "The baby's coming!"

"Yes!"

In the background, Ally heard Elizabeth grunt, then some muffled noises, and then Adam got on the phone. "We're headed to the hospital now, but I'll keep you updated on the baby's progress. You can reach us at this number."

"Okay!" Ally suddenly didn't know what to say. "Good luck!"

"Thanks, I think I'll need it," Adam said, but she could hear Elizabeth say, "*You* need it? I'm the one pushing a human being out of my body!"

Ally imagined the scene with Adam and Elizabeth, wishing she was there with them. She got up from the bench and ran back to the patisserie. She needed to ask for some time off. She could probably catch a flight out that weekend and stay for a few days. Then she could spend time with the baby. And her parents.

And maybe Michael.

"You can't take any more time off," Chef Emile said, shaking his head.

"What do you mean? I have time, still."

"You just returned from a trip."

"I took family leave. My father had a heart attack."

"Non."

"But I have the time."

"But you will not have a job when you return." Chef Emile crossed his arms against his chest. "I'd like you to make an extra two dozen tartes for tomorrow. It's going to be a busy day."

As she walked back to her station, her phone started blowing up with texts from everyone in the family. A group text with all of her cousins, her aunts and uncles, and her parents. All talking about going to the hospital, making up a meal plan, and who was going to take care of the animals. She turned off her ringer and set it on the counter.

She was going to miss it.

～

"What a shame," Frank said as he read from his phone screen.

"What's a shame?" Michael asked, wondering if everything was okay with Elizabeth. The morning started with the announcement of the baby's arrival, and Frank and David had been on edge all day.

"Ally won't be able to make it for the baby."

"What?" David picked up his reading glasses from the desk and read the text. "Oh, that is a shame."

Michael thought the same. He had hoped she'd come back. Then he'd be able to talk to her, tell her what he'd tried for weeks to write in a letter.

He missed her.

He missed everything about her.

But maybe it was better if she didn't come back. That way he wouldn't have to ask her to give everything up. Get stuck in Camden Cove, and let her dreams fall apart.

"She's going to be so disappointed."

Michael knew that not being able to come back for Elizabeth would kill Ally. Another big moment she wouldn't be a part of, another degree of separation between her and her family.

"It's probably that nasty new chef who took over Jean-Paul's position." Frank leaned over the counter and grabbed a truffle from the tray Michael had just finished. "I still can't believe they passed her up for that position."

Michael stayed quiet, but he couldn't believe it either. When he had heard that she'd been passed up, he couldn't believe she stayed. She was more than qualified to run a bakery, even if it was some fancy, well-to-do Parisian bakery. She had more talent than most. What wasn't said, but was clear, was that Jean-Paul didn't even consider her.

Which said everything about Jean-Paul.

David set his phone down and went back to his computer. "She shouldn't have stayed so long when I had the heart attack. I had a feeling she wouldn't be able to just come back when the baby came."

"What a shame," Frank repeated as he grabbed another truffle.

"Hey." Michael pulled the tray away and put it in the refrigerator. "I don't have time to make another tray. I'm going to see my mom this afternoon."

"Sorry." Frank made a face. "I need chocolate today."

"Why don't you bring all the day-olds to the nursing home with you?" David got up and grabbed the attention of one of the dishwashers. "Collect what's left out on display and package everything up."

"That would be great."

When Michael left, he thanked David and told Frank to keep him updated on the baby. He drove down toward Majestic Oaks, but wished he had time to switch to his bike. He didn't really want to think. And he didn't want to remember Ally wrapping her arms around him.

"Well, my goodness!" Loretta exclaimed when he dumped all the boxes of baked goods onto the recreation table. "This is going to be a treat. Robert, did you see what Michael brought?"

Michael looked at his mother, who sat in the chair next to the window. She looked out to the garden, where the residents rarely were able to spend time. She watched as a hummingbird ate from a feeder.

"Hi, Mom." Michael set her favorite, a strawberry macaron, on the table next to her chair.

She didn't look away from the bird. "It glistens in the sun."

He remembered all the feeders she had up in the yard when he came back from deployment. There were at least half a dozen in the yard, all empty, all forgotten. It was his first sign that things were not okay with her. Usually, she would've brought them inside for the winter because of the bears, but they hung or lay on the ground, not taken care of for some time.

"The only bird that can fly backwards, right?" he said, remembering what she had told him as a boy.

She didn't respond to him, just watched as the bird flew away.

"What's that?" she asked, pointing to the pink macaron.

"That's your favorite." He picked up the treat on its napkin and handed it to her.

She swatted it away. "I don't like those."

He almost lost the cookie to the floor, but caught it in time. "It's a strawberry macaron. You used to love them."

"Do I know you?"

His jaw clenched and he squeezed the cookie in his hand. He couldn't do it. He got up, throwing the macaron in the trash on his way out of the rec room, not even acknowledging his mother's question. He just couldn't do it.

Loretta followed as he headed down the hall. "Everything okay?"

He shook his head. "I got to go." He felt suddenly ashamed of his behavior.

"You know, she's happy."

"What?" He appreciated Loretta, but he didn't believe her. How could anyone be happy with losing their mind?

"She isn't tortured, like a lot of the others. She seems content in the present moment, like watching the birds, or sitting with the others in the room. Sometimes she even enjoys talking about Chicago with me. The hardest thing about this disease with women like your mother, is the people watching them live with it." She gave Michael a hard stare. "You're the ones who lost the time. You can't lose what you don't remember."

He glanced back to the rec room. His mom was sitting still, looking out the window at the bird feeder. "I know nights are hard for her."

"Yes, but we help." She put her hands on her hips. She looked like she was thinking something over in her head, then said, "I have spent enough time with Rose to know, she wouldn't want to get in the way of someone's life," Loretta said, not at all deterred by Michael's silence.

He wished he'd driven his bike. "Have a nice night, Loretta."

He headed for the exit, leaving before hearing what else she had to say. He didn't need to hear anymore. She was right. Of course. His mother wouldn't want to get in the way.

It had always been him in his own way.

Harry, Frank and David, and now Loretta thought he was being the typical Michael, the guy who stuck to himself, didn't let people in, miserable S.O.B. If they knew he gave it all to her, almost every ounce of him, and she still didn't want him, then maybe they'd lay off him.

She grabbed her bag and left her apartment. Samir would be there soon to pick her up. She had another cooking class with the group. This time she was going simple – a loaf of crusty French bread.

Dorothy greeted Ally at the front door to her apartment with the traditional kiss on both cheeks. "Did you have any trouble?"

Ally shook her head, Samir carrying her bags on his shoulders. "None at all."

"Samir, would you please bring it all to the kitchen." Dorothy waved a hand for Ally to follow.

The first thing Ally noticed about Dorothy's apartment was that it looked like something from out of the movies. It was exactly what one would imagine when thinking of Paris. Fifteen-foot-high ceilings, fishbone parquet floors, with balcony doors overlooking the City of Light. The place was mostly classic French décor, but modern pieces sat among the antiques. Most of the artwork was abstract with bold colors.

"You can see the Eifel Tower from here." Ally stopped to admire the structure from the window.

Dorothy looked out at the view. "I've never gotten used to seeing that outside my window."

"I love seeing the energy from the city," Ally said, watching the people below on their way through the city streets.

"Yes, there's something about the energy, the pulse, beating creativity, thought, and reflection that happens everywhere in Paris." Dorothy floated her hands out before her like a composer, her cane resting by her side. "There's beauty, there's history, there's everything!"

Ally understood. She did. But she still felt something was missing.

"Let's get you set up!" Dorothy rubbed her hands together and led her to the kitchen. If the living room was an indication of the rest of the house, Ally shouldn't have been surprised when she walked into the kitchen, but her mouth dropped open anyhow. White marble covered almost every surface, except the stainless-steel appliances. White marble floors, white marble counters, and white marble backsplash. Every utensil and kitchen appliance she could've dreamed of sat in a perfectly placed position. It was a chef's dream.

"This place is beautiful."

"I hope you enjoy it, I've always wanted a kitchen where I'd be able to create something for friends and family." Dorothy's proud smile faded. "But all my kids have grown and moved away, unfortunately. Now I only have Paris."

Sadness filled her eyes as she studied the pristine white kitchen. It looked as though no one had used it recently, which broke Ally's heart. "Would you like to keep me company while I set up?"

"That sounds fabulous." Dorothy pulled out a stool from under the counter and sat down. "Samir, would you mind terribly making us a cup of tea before you go?"

"Of course not." Samir filled the kettle with water. He obviously knew his way around the space, as he went about his business making tea, grabbing the bags from a glass jar, pulling two mugs from the cupboard, and taking cream out from the fridge. When the kettle hissed, he poured one cup and handed it to Ally, then fixed the next cup with a splash of cream and gave it to Dorothy.

"Thank you, my darling." She kissed him on the cheek as he walked out of the room.

He waved. "I'll be back to bring Ally home."

"Thanks, Samir," Ally said.

"You're welcome."

Ally pulled out one of the two standing mixers from each bag. "Thank goodness Samir is so strong," she said, thinking about how he'd carried them from her third-floor apartment and all the way to Dorothy's.

Dorothy looked over at the machines. "Yes, he's the greatest."

"How did he start helping you?" Ally still wasn't exactly sure of their relationship. Was Samir just a neighbor, or was he hired help as well?

"He played the piano for one of my parties, and I couldn't believe how talented he was. Then he told me how he'd have to leave the city because he couldn't find work."

Ally thought of Samir's tall stature and physique. The idea of him playing the delicate keys made her smile. "Really?"

"Yes, a brilliant pianist." Dorothy shook her head then said, "But no one was hiring him, except for a few venues here and there. That hardly paid him anything, so I offered him a job as my assistant, and it ended up working out for both of us. He helps me manage my properties, brings me to appointments, and helps around the house. He's become quite a friend, as well."

"How nice that it worked out for both of you." Ally pulled out the containers of flour and sugar along with the measuring cups and spoons. "Do you mind if I use the island for the demonstration?"

Dorothy wiped her hand over the smooth surface. "No, I think that would be perfect."

Ally nodded, wishing Michael was there with her. The energy she felt teaching with him never seemed to fully replenish itself since she left Camden Cove.

"Do you need anything else?" Dorothy asked, getting up from her stool. "I'm going to freshen up before everyone arrives."

Ally looked at the clock. She had about half an hour to finish up the prep work, which was more than enough time. "I'm all set."

Dorothy left and Ally continued to busy herself, setting things up, then rearranging them. She was distracted. She hadn't heard from anyone about the baby. The group text hadn't been updated with any news, which meant they'd either created a new one, or there wasn't any new news, or they were all together at the hospital, so they didn't need to send out a text about it.

Maybe there wasn't any news. Babies took a long time. She'd heard of people being in labor for days. Maybe Elizabeth was one of them.

They wouldn't forget to call her and tell her she had the baby, right?

She picked up her phone and called Frank.

"It's a girl!"

"What?"

"It's a girl, Elizabeth and Adam had a baby girl. Just beautiful. Perfect!"

"When?" Her heart fell to her stomach.

"About an hour ago."

"Nobody called me," her voice cracked. *Ugh, please don't start now.* She wiped the tear about to fall.

"She's still getting settled, she'll call you when she can," Frank's voice softened.

Ally didn't care if she sounded selfish. Elizabeth didn't need to call her. Just someone.

She had been forgotten, again.

CHAPTER 19

$\mathcal{A}$lly sat at the end of the bar with Margot, who talked animatedly to two men who had just bought her a drink. Ally declined, but thanked them. She was too busy scrolling through rental properties outside of Paris.

"Why would you want to leave the city?" Margot asked, as if she was mad to even consider it.

"There's a small patisserie for sale in Normandy, in the center of town. The idea of living in a small village seems kind of nice."

"Stay in a village with nothing to do, so you can bake what you want?" Margot shook her head at the man standing next to her. "You have a good job, baking at La Michalak. Why would you want to give that up?"

One of the men sat down next to her. "I'm from Normandy. It's quite beautiful, but it's not Paris."

"Maybe I'm not supposed to be in Paris?"

Margot wrapped her arm around Ally and said, "Nous aurons toujours Paris."

"Yes, we'll always have Paris." The horrible last words of Jean-Paul.

She closed the screen on her phone and ordered a glass of red.

The man next to her pulled out his wallet to pay, but she shook her head and the bartender handed her the receipt.

"A feminist."

"Her heart was recently broken."

"Ah, a broken heart does better with a glass of Armagnac." His thick accent slurred his English words together. "Four Armagnacs for our friends!"

Ally didn't protest, though, she didn't need it either.

The night ended with Ally saying good-bye to Margot and her new friends and heading back to her place. As she walked up Rue Lamarck, she couldn't help but admire the French architecture. The golden stone exterior was ornate, with iron balconies hanging over the sidewalks, flowers dripping from window boxes, each building unique, yet with a cohesive style.

When she reached her apartment, she went directly to the computer and looked again at the small bakery in Normandy.

It would be perfect. Perfect spot, perfect space, perfect time. Yet, something nagged her about leaving. It was exactly what she'd turned down with her dads. It wasn't her dream. It was conceding that she wouldn't make it in Paris.

She didn't want to settle, either.

She'd just have to keep looking.

Michael pulled the van up behind the restaurant and opened the back doors. On the floor in the back was the first official wedding cake he had created all on his own. It was the one thing David hadn't fully relinquished to Michael. But he had finally convinced Frank it was best for the bakery. If they wanted him around, then he'd have to do more than just the day-to-day baking.

Frank helped pull out the boxes from the back. "She's perfect."

"What's her name?"

"Sarah, after Elizabeth's mother."

"That's a great name."

Michael always thought he'd have a Rose. However, in order to do that, he sadly recognized two things. One, he'd have to have someone in his life to have a baby with, and two, his mom wouldn't know anyway. He was too late.

"Let's bring the cake into the kitchen, and then I'll set up the coffee bar."

Michael had no idea what kind of energy David had put into the wedding side of things until today. The cake was a feat in itself, but that was the easy part. David was known for was his coffee bar. Biscotti, cookies, finger tartes, scones, and more, would be served with the coffee. Not only did David bake over a dozen different types of pastries, but different varieties of each. Almond, meringue, lemon, chocolate, and other flavors he had never thought of. Michael had never baked so much in his life. He couldn't believe David had done this on his own for so long. He was exhausted, and he still had the rest of his regular baking to do after setting up the wedding.

As Frank decorated the table, Michael put the finishing touches on the wedding cake. The seven-tiered cake took on the traditional Austrian Sacher torte, and made it as decadent as the lavish wedding. Seven layers of chocolate with raspberry filling, covered in chocolate buttercream and topped with chocolate ganache. It was a work of art.

"You should take a photo and send it to Ally," Frank said.

Michael was thinking the same thing, but didn't actually think he'd do it. "She's baked cakes like this, I'm sure."

"But you haven't." Frank carefully arranged the scones in an antique porcelain bowl.

He took a step back, looking at the finished product. He took a picture, but not for Ally. For himself. This feeling, this was why he baked. This feeling of fruition, of fulfillment. But as he looked down at the image, something felt off. He *did* want Ally to see.

Screw it.

He held his thumb on the image and typed quickly, hitting send before he could regret anything.

It's done.

His phone dinged before he even had a chance to put it away in his pocket.

It's beautiful. Well done!

His thumbs hovered over the keyboard, afraid to type, yet didn't want to wait another second to hear from her again. This could be the door he needed to open. Maybe she felt something missing, too?

But what should he write?

That he missed baking with her? How he missed hearing her voice and smelling her scent as she worked next to him?

"I think she and Jean-Paul broke up," Frank said it as though he had read Michael's mind.

So, it was true.

"She hasn't officially told us yet, but she hasn't mentioned him in weeks." Frank shrugged. "Apparently she's mad at us again."

Michael thought back to when she had sent him her new address. Did she keep that information to herself so he wouldn't get any ideas? "She's not mad at you. She just doesn't feel a part of things, that's all. She feels left out, being in Paris"

Frank shook his head. "We all forgot to call her when Elizabeth's baby was born, and I know her feelings were hurt. She said she was fine, but she's avoided our calls since then."

He knew Ally must have been devastated, especially with not being able to come back. Frank looked at him, like he might have the answer, but Michael was the last one who understood Ally. "Ouch."

"I know, I feel horrible." Frank's face drooped. "I don't think she's going to get over this one."

Frank looked at Michael, waiting for his reply. Michael let out a moan. He didn't want to get involved, but with the way Frank looked, he couldn't back out. "When was the last time you went to visit her?"

Frank looked surprised by the question. "Not for a while. Do you think she wants us to come out?"

"Yeah." Michael couldn't believe he hadn't thought of it before. But that's exactly what she wanted. She wanted someone to visit her.

"Well, I don't know if David will be able to, with his recovery and all." Frank tapped his finger on his jaw. "I guess we could ask his doctor when we can travel."

"She just wants to be part of things."

Frank looked as though he was about to say something more, but was interrupted by the wedding coordinator.

He glanced down at her message. Then began to type.

Frank feels bad about the baby.

The bubbles reappeared.

He should.

He couldn't help but smile. He could see her having a pout about it. Rightly so, but still a temper tantrum.

Still a princess I see, he typed, and sent it.

That's right, Holden Caulfield.

He was about to argue, but suddenly saw his teenage self through her homecoming queen eyes and realized she was right. He had been a pompous, holier-than-thou, angsty kid.

God I'm annoying.

Her bubbles flashed across the bottom of his screen.

Apparently I'm dramatic...

He laughed out loud. Then he switched gears, and letting go a bit more, typed, **How's the new digs?**

Small, but perfect for me.

She wasn't going to say it, but he wanted so badly to know. Where was Jean-Paul? He thought of all the different ways he could ask, but if she wasn't willing to tell him, then he shouldn't overstep.

How the cooking classes going?

Good, but...

The bubbles appeared again. But what? He wondered if the new place was too small. Did she have to find a new place?

I miss having an assistant.

Shoot. He stared down at the phone. What the heck did that mean?

~

She couldn't have been more clear in her text. She missed Michael. There. She'd said it. But when his reply didn't come, she felt as though maybe she wasn't clear enough after all. Had she insulted him in some way?

She typed furiously into the phone, writing everything that came to mind in one long paragraph. She wrote about how much she missed being in Camden Cove, but only because of him. How she didn't realize how much she'd miss him until she left. How she hadn't stopped thinking about him since. But as she read over it, she hit the delete key and erased every single word.

Would she leave Paris?

Non.

And that was the end of it. Maybe her pride was too big. Maybe she was too full of herself. But she couldn't leave. Not now. Not when her dreams were so close.

And if she wasn't willing to give it up for him, how could she ever ask him to give everything up for her?

She put the phone down and stood. She walked to the window and looked out at the lights across the street. Each lit apartment had a completely different world inside it. Michael had a completely different world, with the bakery, and his mother, and his close friends. He couldn't and probably wouldn't leave, which was exactly why Ally couldn't ask that of him, because she already knew the answer.

Was she really thinking of his thoughts and feelings?

Was she purposefully jeopardizing it so that it wouldn't come back to hurt her?

Or was she just being selfish?

The next morning, she couldn't shake the horrible feelings in the pit of her stomach when nothing, no reply at all, came from Michael. She couldn't believe how rattled she was by the whole thing. Here she was, thinking she had broken his heart that night when he tried to kiss her, but he certainly didn't miss her enough to say so.

"Did Michael text you that picture of the cake?" Frank asked over the phone later that day.

"Yes, the wedding cake." It looked like one of David's cakes. Michael clearly had no trouble replicating her father's complicated French recipes. He certainly didn't need to be someone's assistant.

"It was a Sacher torte," Frank said.

"Great pick for the season." She thought of Maine's wild raspberries growing alongside the roads.

"Yes, he's really talented, that one." Frank sighed. "You know... he's..."

"He's what?"

"He's been quieter."

"He's always quiet."

"No, I mean, he's lonely."

"He should get a dog." She didn't want Frank to start involving himself now.

"I think he misses you."

Ally pressed her lips together so she wouldn't shout back at him. "I should let you go. Thanks for calling, though."

"Ally, we were thinking of coming out. David's doctor suggested we wait a bit, but we could start planning a good time for when we get the go-ahead."

Ally sat up, surprised. She looked around her tiny space. "Sure."

She could stay at Margot's and give her dads the apartment.

She could even ask Dorothy to stay in the maid's quarters off the kitchen.

"Well, good. We'd love to come to stay for a bit, see what it's like to be Ally!"

She smiled, liking the idea. Liking it very much. "I'd love that."

CHAPTER 20

*A*lly just pressed his number. No more thinking about it. It was early, but she knew he'd be in the bakery already. And if she didn't get this off her chest, she would lose more than one night's sleep. Why did she send that text without thinking first? Another foot in the mouth, but she may have done worse, like insulting him.

By the fourth ring, she almost hung up when he finally answered. "Hello?"

Did he not know who was calling? Was her number not in his phone any longer? Was it not him? "Michael?"

"Ally?"

"I didn't mean that you should only be an assistant. I meant to say that... that..." The words had stumbled out of her mouth. But now she couldn't get them out. She took a breath. "That I missed... cooking with you."

He stayed silent. And the longer he stayed silent, the more she feared that she'd blown it. Again.

"I'm sorry if I insulted you by saying I missed having you as an assistant."

"You didn't."

"Oh."

"So, that's all?"

"What do you mean?"

"That's all you wanted to talk to me about?"

She thought about all the things that had been happening. Did he want to hear about her life falling apart? Then her nerves started in again and she blurted out, "I think I'm going to open a bakery in Paris."

"Wow, that's great."

"You're the only one I've told so far."

"Oh."

Silence again. "I haven't been able to find a space yet in the city."

"Be patient." His voice sounded sincere, like the old Michael, the one who liked her for who she was.

"I wish..." She stopped before she said anything more.

"You'll need an assistant," he said.

"I didn't call because I wanted you to be an assistant." Did he think that was what she was telling him?

"No, I didn't think that, but you'll need help. I honestly don't know how David put in all that time by himself."

She thought about her dad. How he gave up his dreams of Paris to move closer to her, but ended up being too busy to see her. She'd spend the afternoons in the kitchen with him after school as he prepped for the next day, but he was never the dad who took her to the beach or hung out at the movies.

Did she want that for herself? Someone who was too busy for a family?

"I didn't mean to say you couldn't do it," Michael said.

She shook her head as though he could see her.

"I know." She let out a sigh. When did talking on the phone become so difficult? "I should probably let you go."

"Are you at work?"

"No." She thought about her new shift. It seems as though asking for another vacation showed her lack of commitment.

"Well, then you should be looking for a kitchen, instead of worrying about me."

Michael said it as though it was the easiest thing to do.

"It's different here." She thought about how it had been four days since the real estate agent called her back. "The pace is slower."

"You've got to keep trying." He didn't let her speak. "You're *really* that good."

"What?" She hadn't meant to ask. But the idea that Michael thought she was really good meant a lot.

"You can't give up."

She could feel a frog form in her throat, clogging her words. "I won't."

She wanted to say so much more. She wanted him to come out and bake with her. She wanted that kiss. She wanted him.

"Now, I better let you go before David shows up."

"He's still coming this early?"

"Your dad has a hard time letting things go."

"That he does."

"Good luck, Ally."

"Michael?" She wanted to say it. She really did.

"Yeah?"

"I've missed you."

Michael told Harry the whole story, sitting in Harry's office.

"So, what did you say?"

"I said, 'oh'."

"You said, *oh?*" Harry's eyebrows lifted. "Are you kidding me?"

"Do you think I'd joke around, when I'm acting like a twelve-year-old girl?"

Harry contemplated it for a moment and nodded his head in agreement. "Good point."

"What do I do?"

"You have to think big, here."

"Like how?"

"Like tell her how you really feel."

"Oh my God, I have to act this way with her, too?" Michael sat on one of Harry's stools, holding his head between his hands. "I can't say this stuff over the phone, not being able to see her."

"Then go to her."

"Go to Paris?"

"You fought in a war zone, and you're afraid of a French city?"

"I'm not afraid of the city."

Harry rolled his eyes. "She called me."

The conversation was going in too many different directions. He wasn't sure what Harry was saying. "She called you?"

"Yes, to ask about Eve. I think she was really fishing for info about you, though."

Michael didn't want to hear this. He couldn't go there. He couldn't. "It's just not a good idea. Her life's over there, and my life is here."

"She won't know."

"What do you mean she won't know? Why go see her, then?"

"No, I mean your mom. She won't know, Michael." Harry's eyes shifted. "I could go and visit her."

Michael looked at his friend. "You'd do that?"

"Of course." Harry opened a box, pulling out books from inside. "I did, while you were away before."

"I can't just up and leave." Michael stood, pacing the small area. "There's the bakery. The house. I can't just leave her, whether she knows who I am or not."

"Look, Frank and David owe you a vacation, as far as I'm concerned." Harry dumped books on the counter. "But beyond that, you owe it to yourself to see if this is real or not. Because sitting in my bookshop talking about girls is worse than behaving like a twelve-year-old, because you're a grown man who's too chicken to find out."

"I'm not chicken." Michael crossed his arms in defense. He

wasn't, was he? "She misses my friendship. If she wanted something more, then—"

"She wouldn't have stopped," Harry interrupted. "I know, you've told me. It doesn't change the fact that the French guy is gone, she's calling you, and telling you she misses you."

Michael just stared at him.

"Go."

"Go to Paris." Michael shook his head.

Harry threw *In Search of Lost Time* at him.

"That many people read Proust?" Michael held the hardcover, thinking of the one he sent to Ally. Had she ever read it?

"You bought the last one." Harry continued to empty the box.

Michael looked through the titles but didn't see anything interesting. He had no idea what to send her, if he wanted to send her something. He couldn't keep sending her stuff. No, he couldn't keep going on like he had been.

Todd and Miles had the whole cooking class, including Ally and Samir, over for dinner. She brought a basket of desserts, things she hadn't made since she was in Camden Cove. Turnovers, donuts sprinkled in sugar, and pastry puffs with crème spilling out of them.

The afternoon had been one big therapy session with her and the dough. She pounded it, threw it on her one square foot of work surface, and pushed it in as hard as she could with her palms.

Michael hadn't said anything. Nothing. The faint "Oh" was it. And she wasn't even sure he meant it to be audible.

She *was* a princess, thinking there might be something still on his end. Glad she hadn't been face to face with him like she had planned, if she went back to see the baby.

No, she was glad she had baked all day, getting over whatever this was, and now knocking on her new friends' door in Paris.

"Bonjour!" Miles said, as he answered her knock. His and Todd's apartment reminded her of her own. Small, narrow, but full of character.

"Salut!" They kissed, and she greeted Todd the same way.

"For dessert." She handed over the basket. "Everyone's here, it looks like."

They were all standing in the living room as music played in the background. This was the kind of night she had dreamed about. A community of people she helped create with her pastries.

Todd handed her a glass of wine and she stood next to Samir, listening to the conversations.

"Pourquoi si triste?" Samir asked. His big brown eyes saw right through her.

She smiled, but she didn't fool him, as his expression didn't change.

"I'm trying to figure out what to do with my life."

There, she'd said it.

"Ah." Samir smiled, then said sarcastically, "That's all? So, I'm not the only one?"

She knew that feeling. Working at La Michalak was that feeling. The glass office in the middle of the kitchen showed her day in and day out how far she had to go.

"I want to quit my job and open a bakery." The words gushed out.

"That's a great idea," Samir said.

"But I can't find a bakery, and I can't quit my current job if I don't have work, and I can't work if I don't have a bakery..."

Samir nodded thoughtfully.

"I assume you've talked to an agent immobilier?" Mr. Peters asked, jumping into the conversation.

She nodded. "I either can't afford it, or it's too much space for one baker."

"Have you talked to Dorothy?" Samir asked.

She looked up at Samir. "No, why?"

He looked over at Dorothy, who was talking to Karen and Jamie. "She has properties."

"A patisserie, too?" Ally doubted it.

Samir shrugged. "She has a place right in the city. You could build your patisserie."

She hadn't thought about renovating an existing place. She could create a patisserie the way she wanted. But she'd have to buy all the equipment and furnishings. She didn't have that kind of cash, and she doubted any bank would loan it to her.

She shook her head, being rational. "No, that's not a possibility."

"You could get investors," Mr. Peters said.

"Who'd invest in me?" Ally wasn't trying to feel sorry for herself, but it was the truth. She was an assistant chef. Yes, it was at one of the best patisseries in all of Paris, but that didn't really mean much when no one knew who you were.

"I'd invest in you," Mr. Peters said. "I could even help you with creating a computer system for your orders and supplies."

Ally was speechless. "You'd invest in me?"

Samir then spoke. "Dorothy would definitely help you find a piece of property."

"What are you all talking about?" Dorothy asked from across the room.

"Ally wants to open a patisserie of her own."

"It should have some space for cooking classes," Karen said.

Ally waved her hand to stop the talk. "No, no, no. There's no patisserie."

"Why not?" Dorothy asked.

"For one, I don't have a place." Samir and Dorothy immediately looked at each other.

"Isn't there a spot on the corner of Versigny?" Samir asked.

Dorothy's forehead wrinkled as she thought about it. "It's quite small, but would work for a neighborhood patisserie."

"I couldn't!"

"Why not?"

Ally stood dumbfounded. She was suddenly overwhelmed by the generosity around her. "Because you've already done so much for me."

Todd walked over to her and gestured toward the others. "Look what you've done for us. We have a little community now. We're here to help each other."

Miles clapped his hands together loudly, twice. "Let's eat and figure out a plan for Ally."

Karen swung her arm around Ally's shoulders. "I could help with the counter until you're ready to hire. I've waited tables and stuff before."

"I think you're getting ahead of yourself." Ally held up her palm, pushing her hopes down. The last thing she wanted was to be hopeful. "I don't even have a business plan."

"Come see the place tomorrow," Dorothy said, as Samir pushed her chair in at the table.

Samir said, "I'll pick you up."

Ally shook her head. "I don't—"

"Where's the harm?" Dorothy asked. "I've lived long enough to know the risk isn't the failure, but the regret."

Ally grabbed the back of the chair, trying to keep herself from floating, but it was too late. Her dreams were lifting her up.

"I probably can't even afford it." She squeezed her fingers against the wood, waiting for it all to fall through.

"If you're baking pastries like these," Jamie said, sneaking a puff, "then you won't have to worry about it."

Ally looked out at them, but tears blurred their faces. "You guys are the greatest."

CHAPTER 21

*A*lly met Dorothy and Samir at her lobby's entrance. She couldn't wait to see the bakery. Maybe this would work out. Maybe she'd get her own Parisian patisserie after all. She remembered pressing her nose against the glass of the cases of David's patisserie as a little girl, trying to figure out which treat she wanted to try next. Those had been some of the happiest moments of her life, and soon, she might have her own. Her very own. She'd be a *patissier*.

What would she name it?

She'd always wanted to name her own place something simple, like *Patisseries et Pain*, or something with *La Patisserie* to give homage to David and Frank. Maybe with her own name, *La Patisserie de Ally*.

The morning fog reminded her of fall. Paris' streets were empty when Dorothy and Samir pulled up in the black sedan. Ally jumped in the car before Samir even opened his door. She'd wanted to ask to go last night, but Dorothy looked tired, and Samir took her home.

When they arrived in front of Dorothy's property, she knew exactly which restaurant Dorothy owned. *L 'Echaugette* had been a popular little bistro that had live music on Friday nights. There was a small bar area near the front door. The interior didn't scream patisserie at all, but as soon as Samir opened the door, she knew it would be perfect.

The wooden floors creaked underneath her feet as she walked across to the dining section. A couple of tables sat in the middle of the room, with a long bench across the side wall.

"How old is the building?" she asked. The location was on a side street that locals used to cut through the neighborhood, but made it quaint, and quiet, for being in the city.

"Not too old, 1870, maybe?" Dorothy said. "My husband had a few properties and left them to me after he died. I'm hoping my son wants the properties soon. I'm afraid being a landlord is more work than I'd like, now."

She rubbed her hand along the shellacked bar top all the way to the end, imagining a bright display of pastries. With a little push, she opened the doors to the back. The kitchen was dank and had a lingering smell of grease. A large sink sat up against the back wall. A walk-in cooler that smelled as though something had died inside, had shelves built into the walls. She opened the doors to the oven that was as old as the building and protruded out from the wall, taking up much of the space in the small kitchen.

"How many racks in the oven?"

"Eight."

The checkered black-and-white floor was surprisingly clean compared to the rest of the place. She could definitely keep the floors. The stove, though…

"This is why you can afford this restaurant." Dorothy stood at the back of the kitchen. "It needs a lot of work, which is why the rent is low, but you could do some improvements inexpensively. Samir, we could ask your cousin to come in and do some reno-vations."

Ally circled the room.

"So, what do you think?" Samir asked.

She put her hands on her hips and said, "I'll take it."

Dorothy and Samir smiled at each other. "You'll probably want to replace the stove, as well as the dishwasher."

The dishwasher was pulled out from the wall, a hose hanging into the sink. The walls were covered in papers of hand-written rules and reminders for the staff. Above the door, a stopped clock hung. She opened the back door up to a small alley, expecting to find it filled with dumpsters, but instead it was clean, with chairs positioned with potted flowers for patrons to enjoy the small area.

"It's perfect!" Ally ran to Dorothy, then to Samir, and hugged them both. "I can't believe it's happening!"

"You deserve it, my darling, you deserve it." Dorothy patted her back.

Ally let go and took a step back to see the whole place. "It's perfect."

~

"She asked for you," Loretta said to Michael, handing him the deck and board. "She even said you'd be coming by to play cribbage."

This was unexpected. His mother hadn't had a day like that in so many months, he didn't even remember. But didn't get his hopes up, he knew better than anyone how quickly things could change. That disease pulled no punches.

As soon as he saw his mother, he could tell she was lucid. It was the way she carried herself. She had always been so proud, shoulders back, head high. As he saw his mother sitting in the rec room, he finally figured out who she reminded him of.

Ally.

"Michael!" She stood from her chair, holding out her arms. She balanced herself against the arm rest.

"Ma." He hugged her, squeezing her tiny body. "I heard you want to play some cards."

"Yes, you know you always said I was really very good."

"How about some cribbage?" He set down the cribbage board on the table next to her chair.

"I've been wanting to play." She folded her hands, squeezing them together so tightly that her knuckles were white.

He wondered if she was as scared as he was that she might not have a moment like this again.

"You deal?" she said.

He split the cards and shuffled them in a bridge, tossing each one out in front of her. She collected each as they landed in front of her, and held them tight against her chest.

"I'm not going to cheat."

"You always did," she teased. The old Rose was sitting in front of him.

His heart burned.

"You want to start, or what?" He gave it back like he would've before he left, before she got sick, before she lost her memories.

She peeked at her hand, looking at her crib, deciding which one to keep. "You look like you haven't eaten a fruit or vegetable in years."

He wondered when the last time was that he'd had a real meal. "When was the last time you read?"

"I can't seem to ever find anything I like."

He rolled his eyes, thinking of the dozens of books he's brought to her. "You used to love to read."

"I *used to* do a lot of things."

Touché.

"What book would you read over again for the first time?" she asked, organizing her deck.

The question caught him off guard. This was the kind of question that she used to ask, a deep question that lead nowhere. It used to annoy him. He didn't realize until that moment how much he missed those conversations.

"To Kill a Mockingbird." He didn't even have to think.

She smiled. "You remember when the power went out?"

"You read all day on the porch."

"That was a great book."

He nodded. "A great book."

"Do you remember how your father used to read to us by the fire?"

He didn't. He didn't really remember much about his father except the yelling and screaming, except the day he left. That, Michael remembered vividly. When he looked up from his thoughts, he could see tears forming in her eyes.

"I thought we were playing some cribbage?" he said.

Her eyes returned to her cards. "So, when am I ever going to meet a girlfriend?" she asked. "You're not hiding anything from me, are you?"

He shook his head. "No, ma, I'm not hiding anything."

"What's the problem then?" She leaned over the table and touched his cheek with her free hand. "You're so handsome."

"She lives in Paris."

Rose's gaze went to him, but she didn't say anything. She looked out the window. "I don't want to be your burden."

Michael could feel the air shifting. He'd upset her. "No, you're not a burden."

She nodded, but didn't look at him. "Then what's holding you back?"

He didn't want to tell the truth, because he may have used his mother as the excuse, but the real reason was him. What if she couldn't love the real him?

She tilted her head, trying to get better eye contact from him, but he couldn't risk her seeing the truth. "You might not get a second chance."

"It's not that simple." He shifted in his seat, trying to focus on his hand.

She shrugged and played her first move. As he went, she looked out the window, her eyes wandering to the gardens.

"Joey, are you ever going to take me home?" she asked.

Joey was his uncle's name. He knew there was a resemblance, something she had told him his whole life, so it shouldn't have ended the moment, but he knew it was over.

"Nope."

How could he leave Camden Cove? How could he leave his mother?

Her eyes flickered around the rec room. They had changed before he even noticed. Confusion and fear set in. "Do I know you from Chicago?"

He shook his head. "No."

Ally moved all the wheeled racks by the sink, then grabbed her rag and wiped down the walls. Grease dripped down as she scrubbed with the hot, sudsy water. Her arm was already sore from the day's work, but she couldn't stop. She wanted to start baking as soon as possible.

The rent was doable. She had been careful to save, put away as much as she could, so she knew she'd be able to get by for at least a couple months without making any money. The equipment and renovations were not something she could really afford, but she knew it had to be done. She would need a lot of patience. It would take time to build what she wanted. But she looked forward to the journey.

When her arm finally became numb, she decided to take a break. She picked up her phone and went out front, sitting at a table. Her dads would be home from the bakery by now. Michael had been closing up, from what they had told her.

She video called, and on the third ring, Frank answered. "Well, hello! This is a nice surprise."

Ally looked for David. "Where's dad?"

"He's sitting in his chair." Frank turned the screen to her dad.

"I have something to tell you guys." She couldn't wait. She stood, flipping the camera toward the room.

"Where are you?" David said, looking over his readers.

"I'm in *my* patisserie!"

"That's La Michalak?" Frank made a face. "It's dirty."

"No, *my* patisserie." She panned the room with her phone. "It's mine. I'm opening my own patisserie!"

She looked back at the screen. David and Frank's mouths dropped open.

"It's yours?!" David laughed. "That's wonderful."

"I thought you said it was dirty."

"It is," Frank said.

"I think behind the walls it's brick." Ally pointed to where the drywall broke behind the bar. "But look at the oven!" She walked into the kitchen and pointed the phone at the floor-to-ceiling oven. "It has eight racks."

"Eight!" David said. "In a place that size? It'll take you all morning to heat it up."

"What are you going to name it?" Frank asked.

"I don't know." Ally kept changing her mind. "I think something like Pain et Patisseries."

"You should have your name."

"Not very French, *Ally*."

"You're right, you're Parisian now."

Ally could feel her belly do a flip-flop as she looked around the kitchen, seeing all the things that would make it great, like the large sinks and shelves along the walls. Things were really happening.

"Have you already left La Michalak?"

"No." Ally figured out she would have to work a little longer in order to do what she wanted. She'd work during the day and renovate at night. She didn't want to take longer than six weeks to get things ready enough to at least open the doors. But she also didn't want to open to the public with the place still a mess.

She wished she could ask for help, but she knew they couldn't travel. It would be another few months, the doctor said.

"Do you have a plan for the menu?" David asked.

"How will you design the floor?" Frank asked over David.

"We can't wait to visit!" David said.

"I can't either." Ally really hoped they would.

She really wished she could ask Michael.

CHAPTER 22

*M*ichael's mind hadn't stopped spinning since he came home from his visit with his mother. He showed up at the bakery earlier than he usually did, but he still fell behind with the daily pastries. He couldn't stay organized. He burned half a dozen loaves of bread by not keeping an eye on them, over whipped some dough, and was behind with most of his times.

Luckily, by the time Frank showed up, he had pulled himself together, but either Frank could tell something was wrong, or he needed to tell him something. He did that thing with the overly friendly banter, giving compliments even where none were deserved.

"What's up, Frank?" he asked, just wanting to get it over with.

"Have you talked to Ally?" Frank asked.

He had hoped Frank would drop this fantasy of him and Ally. All it did was keep things spinning in his head. And he was tired.

"No." He could hear his own shortness and regretted it, but kept working. Maybe Frank would take the hint.

"Well, she's bought a patisserie."

Michael stopped what he was doing. "What? She did it?"

His heart swelled with pride for her. *She did it.* "Is she freaking out?"

He knew she would be excited, it was a dream come true, but she would also be worried about something or other.

"I just wish we could go over there and help." Frank looked at Michael. "You should go."

Michael pretended he wasn't thinking the same thing. "I couldn't."

"She'd love the help." Frank obviously still oblivious to the whole situation. "Honestly, it wouldn't kill us to close during the winter for a few months. You'd learn so much. It would be a great opportunity."

Michael let out a deep sigh. "I can't leave unless, well…" He stopped, his eyes suddenly stinging. "This is my only thing right now."

He went back to work, wrapping cellophane over the pastries.

Frank nodded as though he understood what that meant. "You always have a place to come back and bake."

"How are you going to handle this place on your own?" The kitchen, David's heart, Frank's anxiety, he wasn't so sure.

"We'll be better knowing you'll be there to help Ally." Frank's lips curled up. "Plus, the season's almost over. We can manage with someone part time, for a while."

"What will David say?" What Ally would say?

"There are direct flights out of Logan," Frank said. "Don't even think about it, just go. Grab your passport and go."

"Go now?"

Frank stepped up to him and placed his hands on Michael's shoulders, looking into his eyes. "I've never seen Ally happier, than she was with you and I know she left, because that scared her."

Maybe that's why she stopped that night? Maybe Frank was right. Michael hoped Frank was right. He better be right.

"What about tomorrow's prep and everything?"

"Michael, you're going to see our Ally. Don't wait."

Michael pulled out his apron and gave Frank a big hug, patting him on the back. "I'm going help Ally."

"I'll keep bringing pastries to your mother while you're away," Frank offered.

Michael clenched his jaw to prevent the trembling. If it wasn't for Ally, he'd stay in this community. It had been good to him, despite the hardships.

"I'll see you in Paris," Frank said, closing the door behind him.

Michael looked at his bike, holding his helmet in his hands.

He needed to pack.

~

Ally was on her break from the icing station. She had officially been assigned a station after weeks of moving around. She really didn't know why the new head patissier held onto her, since for some reason, he didn't really like her.

Margot took a puff from her cigarette. "You threaten him."

"Hardly."

"He sees your talent, otherwise he'd find someone else. He just wants to let you know who's in charge."

Soon, I'll be in charge, she thought, as she jotted things in her notebook. She hadn't told Margot, worried she wouldn't be able to keep it a secret. She needed this job, whether she wanted it or not. At least until she opened. In her notebook, she wrote a list. She wanted to make a supply list, a spreadsheet of costs, supplies, a computer system for the retail, the exchange of money. Employees. The list kept getting longer and longer.

"Have you talked to Jean-Paul?" Margot twisted her cigarette out in the ashtray.

Ally hadn't even thought about Jean-Paul. She had no idea if he enjoyed his new bakery, if it was even open yet, or if he was doing okay. "Non."

"He was always a connard. Good riddance." Margot shrugged. "You should go home and take a long bath, relax."

Ally didn't say anything, but she wasn't going home. She was headed straight back to her new patisserie. *La Petite Patisserie.* The name came so naturally one night, she almost wondered if she had known it all along.

When her shift ended, she met Samir at the bakery to receive the new refrigerated displays. *Next will be the new dishwasher*, she thought as she watched the delivery men bring in the new appliances. She flipped the lights. The room reminded her a little bit of David's kitchen. A cozy, homey feeling. She wanted people to feel comfortable, to stay and enjoy themselves.

She walked back to the kitchen and filled a bucket with soap and water at the sink. She'd start painting the dining area that night. They had moved the bar to the other end for a coffee station, which opened the whole place up.

But first, she opened up the large roll of butcher paper, rolling it out and measuring it. She taped pieces together, making a huge rectangle to fit the front window display. Then she painted: *La Petite Patisserie. Ouvert tôt!* And hung it in the window. She put no other information on it. No number. No website. No social media. It would be completely organic. She knew how quickly word of mouth would travel, and she knew why this would work.

She could bake.

Really well.

When she finished with the sign, she scrubbed down the dining room walls, scraping off food stains, cleaning the baseboards and floors. It might be old, but she could get it clean and put together until real renovations could be done.

"Do you like it?" Samir asked, pointing out the placement of the displays.

Ally stepped back, determining whether there was enough viewing room. People would linger, look through all the beautiful options luring them to find the perfect treat. "It's perfect."

Samir nodded, then wiped his hands together. "What's next?"

"Samir, I'm good. Go home."

"I'll meet the delivery man in the morning, for the dishwasher."

Ally nodded. "Merci! How can I ever repay you?"

"Dorothy has been a good friend, and I like her being part of something again. She is a beautiful soul, who just needs people around to keep her going, and you're her people."

Ally smiled. She was glad to be Dorothy's people. "I like you both very much."

"I will be away in a few months, I'm hoping you can all pitch in together and take her to appointments if she needs it, until I get back."

"Of course!" Ally could make it work.

"Tomorrow, then."

"Tomorrow."

Samir walked out into the night, leaving Ally alone with her painting equipment.

She turned on her music app, playing something as far from French as she could get, a little country station she'd found. It reminded her of being with Michael. The music he listened to in the kitchen and in his truck. She thought she was too cool for country before Michael, but for some strange reason, now she really liked it.

As the sun crept down behind the buildings, the shadows dragged along the floor as she painted. She'd have to hire soon, get someone to work the counter with her. A Frank. Maybe a kitchen assistant. She'd do the dirty work for the time being, dishes, clean-up, deliveries if there were any. She'd be willing to do what was necessary to keep going.

Then a song came on that had played in the park that night with Eve and Harry. She thought about sitting next to Michael on the blanket, grabbing his arm as they walked through the crowd. She missed him.

She missed him a lot.

$\sim$

Michael looked out the plane's window at Logan International Airport as the plane taxied down another runway, waiting for their turn to take off. He checked the time. Seven hours and he'd be in Paris. No reservation. No immediate transportation. No nothing, but the backpack under the chair in front of him.

What was he thinking? He threw his head against the headrest, closing his eyes.

"First time to Paris?" asked the elderly woman sitting next to him.

"Yes," he said. He looked out the window. He could feel her wanting him to say more. "You?"

"No, I have a son and daughter who live overseas for work." She pulled out her phone and opened her photos. "These are some of my grandchildren."

Michael wished he'd ignored her when he had the chance, but instead, he pretended to look through Madison and T.J. and Natalie's pictures. "You have a beautiful family."

Suddenly the engine revved, and he noticed the speed increasing.

"You know, I've always wanted my family to live close, but I guess you just have to do what you have to do. I'm retired, luckily, but Sandra's parents are still in New Jersey, working."

He figured her incessant talking was a good distractor, because he needed something to distract him. Something to keep his mind off Ally. But as she kept talking, he wished he could casually talk about what he was about to do, without the feeling of vomiting in his mouth.

The plane sped down the runway, his head pushed back by the force, and then there was the familiar swoosh into the air. The plane tilted, and she stopped talking. He looked out at the sun shining off the Atlantic water. It was beautiful. He'd miss it.

But he couldn't wait to leave it behind.

CHAPTER 23

*A*lly only slept and showered at her apartment these days. The moment she woke up, she headed to the La Petite Patisserie. *My little patisserie.* The morning air had a chill. Fall no longer crept around, it was fully in view. Leaves of gold, amber and burgundy dangled off the trees and fell, swaying down to the ground. She walked past the Hausmann buildings, in the shadows of the basilica, hot chocolate wafted in the air as a couple with mugs passed her. The street no longer littered with tourists, but locals in scarves and hats.

She slipped the key into the lock, pressing hard against the handle, a trick she'd already had to learn. The door jammed, but with a good kick, it swung open and she turned on the lights. Each time she stepped inside, she felt the same rush she had the first time she saw the place. She hoped she always felt as happy as she did now.

She finished painting the second coat by lunch, and dumped all her painting stuff in the sink, running water over it. She dug her fingers into the brush, the paint swirling out. She had picked a light gray, something so pale and light it looked almost white. She wanted the color from the pastries to pop. Throughout the day, Frank kept sending her pins on cute little bakeries, and a text came as the oven timer dinged. French bread baked in the enormous oven. She had been practicing all morning. She pulled out a tray of golden crusted bread. They looked perfect.

She grabbed some brie and an apple and sat on the stool next to the counter. She opened the journal Michael had sent her, all of her ideas written inside, her lists, her receipts, her hopes and dreams.

From the front, she heard a man's voice calling out, "Ally! Bonjour!"

She stepped out from the kitchen, expecting to see Samir, who said he might stop by, but Todd and Miles stood inside.

"We got you a present!" Between them was an old board. "We found it at a farm sale in Provence. It's a chalkboard!"

She looked at the board and imagined her menu drawn on it. "It's beautiful!"

"It was used in some barn to write down the planting dates and stuff." Todd held it up. "You could put announcements, or specials, or put it out front to catch customers."

"That's a great idea."

"That yummy magical smell coming from your kitchen definitely will."

Ally walked toward the kitchen and waved at them to follow. "I'm working on my breads tonight."

"Oh my." Todd didn't hide his shock at the size. "I hope you keep Dorothy's place for classes."

"It's a diamond in the rough," Miles said.

"It's a work in progress, definitely, but if you look over here…" She led them out to the front. "You'll see there's plenty of space when the shop is closed." She pointed to the area where she'd planned to put a few tables for customer seating. "I'm thinking of allowing community meetings, like book clubs, and have music on Friday nights. Sell some wine with the pastries."

She could visualize the whole place, even the people sitting inside La Petite Patisserie.

~

Michael stood in line as he went through customs. He hadn't ever traveled as a civilian, except when he went to Pete's funeral. He thought about the two changes of clothes, his one-way ticket, and lack of accommodations. Maybe he wouldn't even need a place to stay. He certainly wasn't going to stick around in Paris if she wanted nothing to do with him.

He'd kill Frank.

He grabbed his backpack by the strap, bouncing on the balls of his feet. He felt very American as the other travelers spoke in languages he couldn't understand.

"Où puis-je vous emmener?" the man behind the wheel said.

"Do you speak English?" he wished he had taken a book of French from Harry's bookstore.

"Oui," he said, but he looked annoyed. "American?"

"Oui."

"Where would you like to go?"

"I'm looking for a patisserie in the 18th Arrondissement, on Rue de la Lune."

The man pulled away from the curb and took off from the airport.

"Do you come for work?"

"No." Michael gazed out the window. "For a woman."

"Best reason to come to the city of love."

He drove toward Paris, the city's skyline visible off in the distance. The drive was only seventeen miles, according to his GPS, but the ride seemed to take forever. Heavy traffic, along with stops and pedestrians, made the ride seem like the longest drive he'd ever taken. His mind kept telling him to turn away, go back home where he couldn't get blown up by her rejection again.

All the signs said he was making a mistake.

But what if Frank was right? And Harry. And Sully. And all the others? What if they were right?

After an hour and a half, Michael arrived in front of a sign written in French. "Excuse me, could you tell me what the sign says?"

"Merci," the driver said, as he received his tip from Michael. "Coming soon. La Petite Patisserie."

"This is it." Michael got out of the car and walked up to the door. An empty basket sat in front of a chalkboard written in French, with tiny drawings of pastries. He pulled on the handle, assuming it would be locked, but the door swung open. He stepped into a long, narrow room with two displays up front, still with cardboard and plastic wrapped around them. A picture window gave off enough light that he could imagine how bright the display cases would be when lit up. Ally wanted to show off her patisseries.

The room was light, fresh, even in the centuries-old building. It smelled of paint and bread.

"Bonjour?" he called out, but didn't hear anyone. "Hello?"

A man and an elderly woman emerged from the back. The woman clasped her hands and tilted her head. "Can I help you?"

He had used up all his French. "I'm looking for Ally Williams?"

The woman smiled. "You must be Michael."

Surprise at hearing his name opened his eyes. "Yes."

"You just missed her." She had an English accent.

"She went to get tools." The man held out his hand. "We're friends of Ally. My name is Samir, and this is Dorothy."

Michael shook the man's hand. "Do you think I could wait?"

Samir nodded. "Of course."

Michael checked out the room. It was narrow and small, but Ally would make it warm and inviting. He could tell she had used ideas from her dads. The bar at the end looked like something they'd do for their coffee station, as well.

"Does she know you're here?" Dorothy asked.

He shook his head. Did she think he was as crazy as he felt at that moment?

"You should see her new dishwasher." Dorothy pointed to the door to what he assumed was the kitchen. Samir led the way, opening the door for them. He walked in and saw that the kitchen was even smaller, with an oven half the size of the room.

"How do you know Ally?" he asked, curious about the pair.

"We took her cooking class," said Dorothy.

Then the two made perfect sense. He looked around the room. Dozens of loaves of bread sat on the counters, all different kinds. Pots and pans filled the sink. Painting equipment was set up around the room, with plastic covering the floors. Ladders, tools, and balled up pieces of tape were scattered around. It looked like a hot mess to anyone who didn't know how Ally's mind was organized, but Michael knew she had it all under control.

~

Ally stood in Monsieur Monreau's hardware store for the second time that day, and the fifth that week.

"I need new rolling brushes." The walls, no matter how much she cleaned them, ruined the rollers. She needed more tape, and rags, *and* paint. He led her down the aisle toward the paint supplies. She'd buy white for the kitchen, classic and clean.

"I'll get your paint started while you pick out your tools."

"Merci."

She grabbed a few different sized rollers, along with rolls of tape. She met Monsieur Moreau up front and paid for her things. Just light enough to carry back to the patisserie in her arms, but heavy enough that she wished she'd taken Samir up on his offer to drive.

But she needed the walk. She needed to think. So much had happened, and she didn't know what had happened first. Her whole life was completely turned upside down in the most wonderful ways, like Alice falling through the rabbit hole to

Wonderland. She felt like any minute she'd wake up and it would all just be a dream.

She did a mental check of her list as she crossed the street. Painting supplies done, now she wanted to finish at least the first coat in the kitchen tonight. That way she could get the dishwasher positioned now that it came in, and organize the equipment.

Then she'd really start baking.

She opened the back door with the bags falling out of her hands, hurrying to the counter to set everything down. There was so much to do! And only the day to do it. Her to-do list seemed to grow as the hours ticked away, and she had no time tomorrow, with work and her cooking class afterwards. She stopped in her tracks when she saw it.

The new dishwasher.

It was beautiful.

Ally walked straight to it. A stainless-steel Bosch beauty. Like the displays in kitchen shows. And again, something inside of her grew, her dream felt even more possible. La Petite Patisserie was real.

She *was* living in Wonderland.

"Hello?"

She turned toward the voice coming from the front. She had left the front door unlocked after people started stopping by. Owners of neighborhood shops came in to check out what she was doing with the new patisserie. But she knew the voice wasn't that of a French shop owner on Rue de la Lune. Her heart leaped. It was American. She had heard it before.

It couldn't be.

She swung the door open and there, standing in the middle of the bakery, was Michael. She didn't move. Her feet were frozen in place. The words came out before she could think. "What are you doing here?"

He rubbed the back of his neck. He was nervous. "I heard you might need some help."

Tears sprung to her eyes. She hadn't realized how much she missed him until he stood right in front of her. She nodded. "What about the bakery?"

He stepped a foot closer to her. "It's still there."

"Did my dads give you a hard time?" She stayed in the doorway.

He took another step closer. "They practically pushed me out the door."

"So, you didn't want to come?" She bit her thumb.

"Ally." He was right next to her.

She looked into his eyes. "Yes?"

"I came here because I missed you."

She swallowed, and a tear fell. "You did?"

He nodded, taking her hands. "And I wish I had told you that on the phone."

"You do?" She stepped out of the doorway, almost touching him.

"And I wish I had kissed you, that night."

"You can."

He let go of her hands, only to wrap his arms around her waist, and kissed her softly on the lips.

CHAPTER 24

"*Au* revoir," Ally said, as she waved the cooking class off for the night.

Elizabeth giggled at something Adam said, as she wrapped her arm in his. They had been using the baking classes as a date night and time away from the kids. Elizabeth had an extra glass of wine and was in full spirits. "Let's hit the book store with Lucy tomorrow, and we'll have lunch on the beach."

"That sounds nice," Adam said.

"It's November in Maine." Michael loved the beach, but the Atlantic wind would definitely blow away their food.

"What are we baking, next class?" asked Norma, a regular of Ally's cooking classes.

Michael looked at Ally. He couldn't remember what was on the schedule. "You'd have to ask the boss."

Ally looked up from talking with another couple who joined the group last week, like she had a sixth sense. "We're baking pumpkin pie."

"Oh, that's right, it's our Thanksgiving here!" Elizabeth said. "Adam can make a charcuterie and I'll bring the wine."

"Just bring yourselves." Ally patted Adam on the back as she walked them to the front of the bakery. "I'll have everything."

"I'm definitely bringing my Susan's green bean casserole, whether you like it or not," Mr. Smith said. He had come to every class since they came back from Paris. Ally had been trying to set him up with Norma for months, but she hadn't managed to get the two to see what she saw, which was they were perfect for each other. "It's not Thanksgiving without it."

"I can make a Parisian version," Michael offered.

"No, no, no. I can make it myself. I just want the canned stuff." Mr. Smith pointed at Ally. "No arguments."

Ally shook her head. "I won't say a thing."

Ally hugged everyone for a second time. A true Parisian goodbye. "Bonne nuit a tous!"

Michael shut the door before all the heat escaped. He switched the light off for the sign. They were officially closed.

"So?" he said, walking toward the kitchen. "Why don't you finish off the wine and eat the rest of those macarons?"

"That sounds wonderful."

He held her hand, blowing out the candles on the tables. There was a random plate and napkin, but he'd clean it up later. The night had gone perfectly. Now, he'd just have to convince her to stay just long enough for him to get home before she did.

He grabbed the bottle of red and backed into the swinging door that led into the kitchen, letting her go in first. "Do you want to turn on some music?"

Her eyes crinkled as she walked over to the speaker, tuning to their station. Soon the familiar twang of some old classic country song played as he poured her a glass and got himself a coffee.

He raised his glass. "To you."

"To me?"

His heart still skipped a beat at her killer smile. "Yes, you."

"Why me?" She clinked his glass, and his head bobbed a nod.

"Because you got Mr. Smith to roll out some dough without it sticking to the ceiling."

"You helped, too," she laughed out, his favorite thing about her. "To us!"

He shifted back to the plan. "How about after I finish cleaning up, I'll head back to my place and make us some dinner?"

"Okay, but I need to finish up some stuff before I come."

He nodded. He knew this was her thing. She liked to stay at the end of the day, planning out the morning and having the place to herself. She was like a little kid planning out a tea party. Sometimes she'd ask him to stay, but most of the time, she'd just ask his opinion over dinner.

During that time, he liked to cook. Big dinners. Steak and potatoes. Chicken wings with buffalo sauce. Chicken and mashed potatoes. None of this omelet with truffles stuff. Dinners a man could eat. Then they'd talk about the next day at the candlelit table.

She might stay late, but besides that, they were at the bakery together, making decisions, renovating and planning the next steps. La Patisserie continued to be a favorite with the locals, but the place had a new renaissance with Ally as the head chef. She had the staples, fresh-brewed coffee, French patisseries, even gourmet sandwiches, but the place had a new vibrant atmosphere. They couldn't keep up, so they hired a couple of workers for the front, and a dishwasher and prep chef in back. They hadn't found a delivery driver yet, but heard from Frank that Bill Garneau's grandson was looking for some extra cash.

After six months of new ownership, La Patisserie was a growing success.

This was good, because Michael loved it. Every Tuesday, they'd take a day off, but he looked forward to going back on Wednesday. He was happy, happier than he ever was.

He jogged down the road, stopping at the corner store, picking up the bouquet he had picked out earlier.

"Hello, Michael!"

"Hey, Louis."

"Did you pick up the ring?" Louis asked.

Michael pulled out the petite diamond ring he had bought with Elizabeth's advice. It was an antique, teardrop-cut yellow diamond. It was the most beautiful diamond he'd ever seen, and Ally had commented about how much she liked it one time while they were window shopping Main Street. It was perfect.

He decided to ask her to marry him when he lost his mom. Loretta had called him in Paris and warned him the end was near. He made it back in time, spending her last days with her, sitting next to her bed, holding her hand, helping her let go. She passed peacefully, just like Loretta had described. No pain, no confusion, or suffering.

Ally flew back to Camden Cove for his mother's funeral. She stood beside him throughout the whole ordeal, held his hand as he buried her, took care of the reception afterwards. The whole community seemed to be in attendance, even in the cold winter rain. Frank and David, along with Sully and his family and Eve and Harry all stood with him as Pastor Meryle gave the eulogy.

After the ceremony the two of them sat in his mother's living room, and that's when Ally turned to him and asked, "What if we ran La Patisserie, together?"

"What about your bakery in Paris?" He couldn't believe she was suggesting leaving after all she had gone through to open it up. "It's your dream."

She took his hands in hers. "It's just Paris, but this." She looked around the house. "This feels like home."

They went straight to David and Frank and made an offer. Dorothy helped sell La Petite Patisserie and they returned home together.

Marriage came up often, but Ally was scared, he could tell. Not that his parents had done it any better. His father lied throughout the whole relationship. Ally frequently talked about the shoe dropping, or the curtain being pulled back from her.

Recently, though, her and her dads' relationship was good, really good. She talked to them on the phone for hours about the patisserie, getting advice and ideas. Frank would frequently call Ally and Michael just to talk.

Michael confided in Ally about his panic attacks, and she'd sit with him when he had them, though they were now few and far between. She encouraged him to see a psychologist and visit a physical therapist about his leg. He wasn't too excited about either thing, but he had to admit they seemed to be doing something right.

What he did do alone, was attend meetings. He continued with his AA group who met regularly at the church.

He was really happy.

And it was only going to get better from here.

Ally stood in the middle of the kitchen and looked out at everything. She couldn't believe it was hers, even after all this time. Owning a bakery had been a little seed of a dream not even a year ago, and now it was a garden blooming, each day the business grew. The bakery quickly turned into a bustling business where locals and tourists alike enjoyed their café au lait along with a sweet pastry.

And they loved the cute couple who owned it.

Besides showing up at her Parisian patisserie, Michael had turned out to be full of surprises. For one, he was really good at working up front. People enjoyed talking to the handsome pâtissier, and he enjoyed them back. He'd talk about each treat as if it were a piece of art, convincing customers to try something new. His passion showed. He also quickly made friends with other business owners in town. The sulky loner of Camden Cove turned out to be the popular one on Main Street.

Another surprise was that Michael enjoyed working the cooking classes as much as she did, if not more. Most nights, they stayed in at his place and talked about baking.

They started looking for places to live, when the time came, something with at least two bedrooms, but she had to admit, she liked the idea of renovating his mom's old New Englander. They didn't need much.

She finished wrapping cellophane around the rest of the croissants and slid them into the fridge to be baked the next day. Turning off the radio, she stopped and listened to the waves outside. She loved hearing the pulse of the ocean. She had heard once that the brain couldn't decipher the sound of traffic from the sound of waves. Paris' sounds had calmed her, but the waves of the ocean allowed her to breathe.

She shut the lights off and left out the back. Pressing the remote button to unlock her new car, she smiled at her Mini Cooper. It was perfect for her, but Michael hated to drive the tiny car. As if his Marine manliness was at stake, or something. But she liked it. It got her through the little town just fine. Like his motorcycle was practical.

She did like riding a motorcycle with him.

She thought of when she'd arrived in Camden Cove. Her life was completely different then. How did Michael overlook her arrogance and snobbery? She still didn't know. Every time she thought of what she'd said about him, it embarrassed her to no end.

How could she have been so judgmental? He was one of the most sincere people she had ever met. He was kind and compassionate. But he didn't need approval from others. If Ally heard a bad review, her whole day was ruined, her mind doubting her skills. He just didn't even give it another thought.

"Who cares?" he always said. "Who cares what others think, if you're putting your heart into it?"

Not that there were many bad reviews. Ally had been very fortunate to receive mostly positive feedback about the bakery. Her classes were a hit, and continued to grow. They even had rave reviews and recommendations when they started to do weddings, which Michael had perfected while working with her dads.

Things were so good, she almost thought she was dreaming.

She drove down Main Street and decided to stop at the store and pick up some things before heading to Michael's. She needed to replenish her first aid kit, after her prep chef had given himself a pretty deep cut the other day. A tub of gelato sounded good for that night.

She got out of her car and walked inside, stopping at the flower display. The bakery could use some fresh flowers.

"Hey, Ally!" Louis exclaimed. "How can I help you?"

"Bonjour, Louis." She picked out a bouquet. "Your Thanksgiving display looks great!"

"Yes." He took the bouquet out of her hands. "You don't need flowers. Michael already stopped by."

"That's funny," she said. Michael and she were really in sync, if he'd already picked up flowers for the shop.

Louis nodded, ushering her out the door. "You should head home."

"But I…"

"I'm closing, so you should just leave."

She didn't know if he was having an off day, or if this was his way of closing, but she was pretty sure he was trying to get rid of her.

"I needed some bandages. What if someone else cut themselves?"

"They'll be there tomorrow. Now go, Michael's waiting for you."

She would never fully understand the people of Camden Cove.

She headed back in her Mini Cooper, her to-do list running through her head as she arrived at Michael's house. She needed to call the laundry service and order more linens for the wedding the following weekend. As she walked up the steps to the back porch, she talked to herself about the prep work that needed to be done before the cooking class the following night. She had all the ingredients from her delivery today.

When she reached the top, she almost didn't notice Michael standing outside the house.

"What happened?" The last time he'd met her outside the

door, he had almost burnt down the place with a grease fire, cooking an Angus steak.

The corner of his lip perked up. "Nothing's wrong."

"Then why are you standing out here?" She looked around to see what she was missing.

"I love you." He grabbed her hands, putting her purse on the ground.

"Aww, I love you, too." Suddenly, the big Marine looked nervous. "Everything okay?"

He blew out a breath. "Yes."

That's when everything went into slow motion. Michael went down on one knee. He pulled out a diamond ring from his shirt pocket. When she recognized the diamond setting, she gasped.

"Yes!"

Michael gave her a look, but had a smirk on his face. "Will you let me ask you?"

"Ask me!" She couldn't contain her excitement, squeezing his hand.

"Allison Sarah Williams, will you marry me?"

She cupped his jaw in her hands. "Yes! Yes! Yes!"

He stood, took her into his arms, and kissed her.

"Shush!" a voice called out from behind the door.

Ally stopped and pulled back to see his face. She heard people. "Who was that?"

The door opened before Michael could answer. Frank poured out the door with David, Elise, and Harry all spilling out after him.

Ally's eyes grew big. "What are you all doing here?"

Frank hugged the two of them into his arms. "We're so happy for you!"

"Michael invited all of us to celebrate your engagement." Elise hugged them after Frank let go. "We're so happy for you two."

Everyone started hugging everyone else on the tiny porch.

"Why don't we go inside and start that celebration in the warmth." Michael gestured toward the house.

As her parents filed back inside, Michael tugged at her hand, holding her back. His fingers brushed her chin, drawing her lips to his, and kissed her.

"I love you, Ally."

"I love you, too."

~

I hope you enjoyed *The Bakery by the Cove*! If you enjoyed this series, please check out my other clean romantic women's fiction series, Prairie Valley Sisters. That series is set in a warm and cozy Midwestern town and follows a family of strong women as they find themselves and some romance with the help of family and friends. Click HERE to read the Prairie Valley Sisters series.

Then, click HERE for a FREE copy of *The Wedding by the Cove*, which is only available to newsletter subscribers. This novella takes you to Zoe and Ethan's wedding, where new love blossoms between Amelia and Ryan! Besides the free story, newsletter subscribers also receive special offers and updates on new releases.

Click HERE or visit ellenjoyauthor.com for more information about Ellen Joy's other books.

ACKNOWLEDGMENTS

Thank you to my amazing editor Katie Page. I'm a hot mess, but you get me and I really appreciate it. I don't know what I would do without you.

Thank you to Zoe Book Design for creating the most beautiful covers. Thank you.

Thank you to my proofreader, my mom, Kathryn Tomaszek. You are the biggest, most loyal reader! Thank you!

Thank you to my amazing and beautiful beta reader, Danielle Thorne. I love you!

Thank you to my family who continue to support me.

Thank you to Kathy Peters, my favorite French teacher. Thank you for helping me!

Thank you to Tina Durham-Bars for proofreading!

Thank you to Teresa Malouf for proofreading again!

Thank you to my readers! Thank you for giving me your time. I know how valuable it is!

ABOUT THE AUTHOR

Ellen lives in a small town in New England, between the Atlantic Ocean and the White Mountains. She lives with her husband, two sons, and one very spoiled puppy princess.

Ellen writes in the early morning hours before her family wakes up. When she's not writing, you can find her spending time with her family, gardening, or headed to the beach. She loves summer and flip-flops, running on a dirt country road, and a sweet love song.

All of her stories are clean romances where families are close, neighbors are nosy, and the couples are destined for each other.

Made in the USA
Monee, IL
15 September 2022

13874401R00142